Miriam Coles Harris

Dear Feast of Lent

Miriam Coles Harris

Dear Feast of Lent

ISBN/EAN: 9783743395169

Manufactured in Europe, USA, Canada, Australia, Japa

Cover: Foto ©Andreas Hilbeck / pixelio.de

Manufactured and distributed by brebook publishing software (www.brebook.com)

Miriam Coles Harris

Dear Feast of Lent

DEAR FEAST OF LENT.

A SERIES OF DEVOTIONAL READINGS,

ARRANGED BY

THE AUTHOR OF "RUTLEDGE," "A ROSARY FOR LENT," ETC.

> "Welcome, dear feast of Lent; who loves not thee,
> He loves not temperance nor authority,
>   But is composed of passion.
> The Scriptures bid us fast; the Church says, now:
> Give to thy mother what thou wouldst allow
>   To every corporation."
>   GEORGE HERBERT.

NEW YORK:
E. P. DUTTON & COMPANY
713 BROADWAY,
1874.

DEAR FEAST OF LENT.

MORNING LITANY.

Jesu, Saviour, God's dear Son,
Now the day has just begun,
Be Thou with us, Holy One,
    Hear us, Blessed Jesu.

Thou who didst at break of day,
Take Thy solitary way,
On the mountain bleak, to pray,
    Hear us, Blessed Jesu.

Thou who lovedst the lily white,
And didst mark the sparrow's flight:
When wakes bird and blossom bright,
    Hear us, Blessed Jesu.

Thou who art the Morning Star
Guard us safe, who pilgrims are
Travelling to the land afar:
    Hear us, Blessed Jesu.

(5)

Rock to shadow weary one,
Shelter from the noon-day sun,
While the day's short course we run,
    Hear us, Blessed Jesu.

Thou who when on earth didst say.
" I must work while yet 'tis day,"
Help us, on our busy way,
    Hear us, Blessed Jesu.

Thou who to Thy breast didst fold
Little ones in days of old,
Keep us in Thine arms safe hold,
    Hear us, Blessed Jesu.

Thou who didst before 'twas light
From the grave's dark lonely night
Upward take Thy glorious flight,
    Hear us, Blessed Jesu.

In that Heavenly Home, with Thee
Day shall reign eternally,
For the Lamb its light shall be,
    Take us there, dear Jesu.

                       A. T. S.

God the Father, God the Son,
Holy Ghost the Comforter,
Ever-blessed Three in One,
  Spare us, Holy Trinity.

Jesu, hear us, Lord of all,
As the shades of evening fall,
Hear Thy servants when they call,
  Hear us, Holy Jesu.

Jesu, born in hour of night,
Lord of Glory infinite;
God of God, and Light of Light,
  Hear us, Holy Jesu.

Thou who on the stormy deep,
'Mid the tempest din didst sleep,
In the gloom Thy servants keep;
  Hear us, Holy Jesu.

Thou whose path was on the wave,
When the winds at night did rave,
Save us, Master, Jesu, save!
  Hear us, Holy Jesu.

Thou whose voice consoling said,
O'er the lifeless maiden's bed,
"She but sleeps; she is not dead,"
  Hear us, Holy Jesu.

Thou who saidst, " I go to end
The sleep of Lazarus our friend,"
Us too waking thus attend,
　　Hear us, Holy Jesu.

Thou who standing by the bier,
Bad'st the mother dry her tear,
Ere the dead Thy voice might hear,
　　Hear us, Holy Jesu.

By the vigil kept by Thee,
In the dark Gethsemane,
When thine own slept wearily,
　　Hear us, Holy Jesu.

Guardian of the soul oppress'd,
Who with still voice murmurest—
" Sleep on now and take Thy rest,"
　　Hear us, Holy Jesu.

By Thy slumber in the cave,
In the deep sleep of the grave,
Guard us sleeping, Jesu save;
　　Hear us, Holy Jesu.

Through the grave and gate of death,
When the faint soul travaileth,
Shelter her thine arms beneath,
　　Hear us, Holy Jesu.

　　　　　　　　　　From THE PRIMER.

ASH-WEDNESDAY.

Blessed are ye that hunger now, for ye shall be filled.—ST. LUKE, vi. 21.

To hunger; to feel actual bodily faintness and suffering from want of food. How few people, born in the ordinarily favored walks of life, ever feel this! It would be quite possible to go from one end of life to the other, and never know this feeling. That is putting ourselves away from our Lord's side, cutting off one of the bonds that tie His children to Him. Shall we not think of this?—He went hungry for us, many, many days. Shall we not go hungry for Him a few hours? One day at a time, patiently? He suffered this, unnecessary evil, it seems to us, voluntarily. We all have the power to suffer it voluntarily. This is just exactly one thing that we can do for Him. In memory of Him; because of our sins, as an act of faith, the reason of which we cannot by searching find out. *Why* is it acceptable to God that we punish our senses, that we put pleasure away from us? There is no answer in nature, in reason, to this. We have God's

(9)

word for it (which ought to be enough). It is not moderation, temperance, that is asked of us. It is actual discomfort, positive (though unimportant) pain. If God had sent us real poverty, it might not have wrought our cure: we might have been bitter and rebellious and taken some means to satisfy our hunger that would have brought us into sin. Many have done this, and we half excuse them, in our thoughts. But God has generously given us abundance; and with this gift, has included another, namely, the opportunity of voluntarily doing this thing for Him. Perhaps He would have accepted it, if it had not been voluntary. We *know* He will accept it, if it is. How strange that He should mercifully bless these little sacrifices, He, who so well knows what sacrifice is! That the rigor of one or two days' fast, and the self-denials of forty others, out of all our year of ease and of abundance, should be acceptable to Him, is very difficult to understand. But that it is acceptable, no one can doubt, who has offered his Lent to God in the right spirit.

Of course if we have prepared our sacrifice, and " put no fire under," we cannot expect to see its smoke rise up to Heaven. If we have begun our

self-denials, little and great, in a spirit of self-re-
venge alone, with no love, and no prayer for love,
of course we shall have our reward, we shall be re-
venged upon ourselves, and that will be all that we
shall be. Or if we have imagined that hardness
of life, without increase of devotion, would help
us, we shall not find our souls much better. Or if
we do it, for custom's sake, blindly, and do not
think about it, doing just as the crowd do, without
thought and affection, we may be a little furthered,
but not much. We shall be missing a great deal,
losing a great "occasion." For it is pretty truly this :
what we put into our Lent, we shall take out of it.
What we sow, we shall reap. In holy offices, they
are what we make them as concerns ourselves. In
the sacraments, they are to us whatever we believe
and desire them to be. According to thy faith, be
it done unto thee. Without thought how unprofit-
able is everything.

Consideration, how often it is urged upon us.
Let us *consider* our fast ; let us sound its depths,
and maybe we shall climb its heights. Let us
remember what it is to fast ; whose command it is ;
who blesses those who heed it ; who it is that loves
a voluntary sacrifice ; in memory of whose manifold

sufferings we offer our insignificant ones ; in what blind faith we have to do it, as without reason and advantage in the light of nature. And let us look to the example of Saints. Let us hear their voice.

———

" Behold these lovers, that with looks elate
    Upon each other gaze ! who may they be
But Francis with his vow'd, his chosen mate,
    His dearest Poverty."

So Dante spake ; " her kind
    First husband dead, she lived withdrawn from sight,
Nor ever thought a second spouse to find,
    A second troth to plight."

" With bare and wounded feet
    She trod the cruel thorns unwooed till now,
For none but holy Francis guess'd how sweet
    The rose-bloom on her brow."

And now a lowly pair
    They dwell content, possessing and possest,
And day by day grows Poverty more fair,
    Grows Francis still more blest.

Yet to a sterner troth
    Than Francis pledged, I bind you, spirits high !
Fear not to plight with mine your spousal oath !
    The bride is ever nigh.

But who her hand will fold
    In his? her form unto his bosom strain?
What heart so tender found, what heart so bold
    To be the mate of Pain?

What eyes can brook the gaze
    Of her wild eyes? what ears can bear the moan
She maketh through dark nights and silent days,
    That she hath dwelt alone?

Yet fear not thou to take
    This woman for thy bride, oh soul elect!
Fear not thy choice, thy pride, thy joy to make
    Of her whom all reject!

Oh! fear not thou to grasp
    Her shrinking form, nor spare for fond caress,
Only within Love's strictest, closest clasp
    Can Anguish learn to bless.

And quail not though she change
    Within thine arms to some foul fearful shape,
Still hold her through each aspect wild and strange,
    And let her not escape!

So shall she turn and meet
    Thy gaze with ardors, transports all her own,
And give, for thine, look, smile and word more sweet
    Than joy hath ever known.

So shall the willing air
    Be wooed with softest marriage peal, the knell
Toll'd for the passing of a long despair,—
    Yea, down to deepest hell.

Its sound will pass, and say,
 Rejoice thou under-world ! a warfare long,
Confused, hath roll'd to victory away,—
 The strong hath met the strong;

Love weds with Pain,—let Sin
 And Death abide, and deem their empire sure,
What now can be too hard for Love to win,
 For Anguish to endure ? "
       DORA GREENWELL.

———

" My sin ! my sin ! O God, my sin !
Lies heavy on this heart within,
All through the dreary live-long day
Wearing my aimless life away,
All through the weary watch of night
Tossing my bed till morning's light,
It lays its heavy load on me,
      Miserere Domine !

My sin ! my sin ! O God, my sin !
Where does its sad account begin ?
Far off in early wasted years
I see it through these dimming tears;
Hence my whole life its clouds attend
With darkening shadow; where the end
Of all this shade and gloom for me ?
      Miserere Domine !

My sin ! my sin ! O God, my sin !
What power shall peace and pardon win ?

What shall blot out the scarlet stain
That doth upon my soul remain ?
What will for me with mercy plead,
For me with Justice intercede ?
Break these sad chains and set me free.
                          Miserere Domine !

My grief ! my grief ! O God, my grief !
Finds in Thy sorrows its relief ;
My soul kneels down by Thy distress,
And, with Thee in the wilderness,
Watching Thy long and patient fast,
Conflict and triumph at the last,
Finds heart to lift its voice to Thee.
                          Miserere Domine !

Thy pain ! Thy pain ! O God, Thy pain !
Is my heart's ease ; Thy loss, my gain.
Thy love in all its depths and heights
These forty days and forty nights
My soul will measure, scale and prove,
Until it learn, itself, to love
And fix its only hope on Thee.
                          Miserere Domine !

Thy fast ! Thy fast ! O God, Thy fast !
Shall thus become my feast at last,
When, through long days and nights of care,
And deep heart-searchings, faith and prayer
Shall take the sins they have descried,
And lay them by Thy suffering side,
And lift their voice and cry to Thee,
                          Miserere Domine !"

FIRST THURSDAY.

THE SERVICE OF SIN.

THE Word of God in a great many places speaks of this service as of a fact: a real condition of things, a bondage of the most actual force. It consists of—1st, a yielding to sin—2d, a living in sin —3d, an obedience to sin as to the director and ruler of our lives. I suppose no one is ever willing to admit that he is ruled by the Devil,—and yet most of us must be,—or the language of our Saviour would have been more exceptional. There are some sins that in others, and even in ourselves, we can see to be ruling, to be setting on fire the whole being. But those are the grosser, greater sins, which even our unpurified eyes can see. Think of the reign of sin within us, which' we do not even recognize. Think of the little impulses so fine and delicate that we have never known we felt them. Think of the multiplied evil promptings that we have never resisted, or made an effort to resist.

It is enough to know this, to think how differ-

ently sin looks to different persons. What is a
frightful sin to a holy, careful soul, is a trifle too
light to be regarded by a person living in a careless,
worldly manner. We see this every day, and know
it, as looking at others. Why is this difference in
respect of the same act or the same thought? The
power of sin, the reign of evil, is in one case broken
by the will, the effort of the person; in the other,
the sinful act or thought is just one of a long train
of harmonious acts and thoughts, in subjection to
the will of the malicious enemy. It fills one with
horror to think of the darkening of the light of conscience by this habitual yielding to evil; of the grad-
ual transfer of allegiance from God to Satan by little
unresisted impulses, little nameless negligences and
indolences. This is a spiritual kingdom, of which
we are warned; and we cannot meet its power by
any but spiritual weapons. Oh! surely it *is* hard—
and the angels and our Lord must feel sorry for us.
For we are body and spirit, and must fight against
Spirit, whose laws we hardly know, whose workings
we cannot see. The vast realms about us, above us,
where only spiritual laws prevail, are so far from us;
there is such a thick veil between. We can purify
our hearts, though, till "every pulse beat true to

2

airs divine;" we can "see far on holy ground if duly purged our mental view." We *can* all this, if we will.

Great God! Keep our faith clear, our will steadfast, our heart diligent, our conscience tender. Help us in our prayers. Defend us ever from our Enemy: in thought, in word, in act. Make us ever to fear him—ever to believe in his tremendous power and watchfulness. And ever to believe in the greater power and keener sight of Him who is pledged to help us if we come to Him and pray.

———

Come and release us, Son of God—
We look for Liberty and Light to Thee:
Thou only sin-bound Souls canst make
　　Imperishably free;

Free from all carking strifes of earth;
Free from the time-forged chains which bind us down;
Free to engage in Faith's high war,
　　To battle for the Crown:

Free from unmanly, selfish aims,
From angry strife of tongues and bitterness;
From crime, oppression, fraud, and wrong,
　　From pride's cold-heartedness.

Free from great Mammon's golden sway;
Free from the wearying thirst for place and power;
From mad ambitions of the heart,
 Which strengthen as they lower:

Free, above all, from inward love
For aught array'd against that Cross of Light
Whose glories, streaming down the world
 Make its dark places bright.

Come and release us, Son of God;
Hope of the Gentiles, SAVIOUR, hear our cry;
Earth wanes toward her evening hour,
 Deliverance is nigh.
     WILLIAM CHATTERTON DIX.

"Oh! let me then in Thee
Be bound, in Thee be free!
A law of death in me
I find, a law in Thee
Of life, that grows to fullest liberty!

Bind Thou this bondman strong
That rules, encroaching long
Where he should serve, and through Thy death and pain
Set Thou the Spirit free
That born to liberty
Still pines! a King that wears a captive's chain!"

FIRST FRIDAY.

———◆———

TEMPTATION.

ST. JAMES tells us to be glad when we are tempted. What is temptation ? And why are we to be glad ? Temptation is one of those things that is inevitable if we are fighting for a place in God's ranks,—it would be impossible to be worth anything and not have endured it. God permits it, therefore it is to be borne. But one thing He does not permit, and that is, that we should fall. If we fall, it is of ourselves ; He that is with us is stronger than he that is against us. But oh ! God must have known what we were made of, and yet His inspired apostle tells us to count it all joy when we fall into divers temptations. If we were all true, all right within, even as a child of Adam can be true and right, it would be possible to count it so. It would be possible to stand up and meet the divers and terrible forms of assault of our malicious enemy, treating them as we treat sorrow, as we treat outside things coming on us unexpectedly. But it is the inward congeniality of the soul with

(20)

the temptation that makes it so horrible. It is the leaning of the flesh and spirit towards the tempter when he speaks, that makes such wild work in people's souls when their hour comes. St. James was not writing of us, I fear, but of his utter Christians in those days of stronger definitions. When people fell then, they fell, Ananias and Sapphira-like; they did not stagger on through a lifetime of half-heartedness.

Well, are these days so dreadful, and is there no way of making them better? Is there no voice from anywhere telling us how to make ourselves so invulnerable that we can count their coming joy? Oh! I suppose the days are not so different, and God has not left us without the chance of standing beside those great and pure souls in the "sweet and blessed country." I suppose that we can be perfect and entire, wanting nothing—at least in God's judgment, though never in our own, and never in man's. *God's measure is such a different one from ours.* I suppose it may be possible for Him to say of such a one as I, Well done, good and faithful servant. To see of the travail of His soul and be satisfied—to love me and see but my love to Him, and my longing to attain His will—my aspirations, not my works, my intentions, not my results. · All these will fall off from me, as the body falls from the soul. All that will live and will be glorified will be—*the love.*

First, St, James says, *patience.* Then prayer. Then faith. Unless we ask in faith we need not think to receive anything of the Lord. St. James is always so practical, so forcible. You have got to have a certain sort of character, either by nature or by grace, or you cannot endure to the end. A whole and entire sacrifice to God, is all that will give you the interior force to withstand the Evil One, and to be able to rejoice at the hot storm of trial. St. James is not an enthusiast, and one always thinks of him as strong and firm, rather than as warm and tender ; but he had found, through his patient, practical way of prayer and patience, this crowning joy of Christian Faith. And we may lay hold upon the hope that it is the *right* of all who practically, simply, and with intention, serve God against the Evil One.

———

What was their tale of some one on a summit,
looking, I think, upon the endless sea,—
one with a fate, and sworn to overcome it,
one who was fetter'd and who should be free ?

Round him a robe, for shaming and for searing,
ate with empoisonment and stung with fire,
he thro' it all was to his Lord uprearing,
desperate patience of a brave desire.

Ay, and for me there shot from the beginning
pulses of passion broken with my breath ;
oh, thou poor soul, enwrapp'd in such a sinning,
bound in the shameful body of thy death !

Well, let me sin, but not with my consenting,
well, let me die but willing to be whole :
never, O Christ—so stay me from relenting,—
shall there be truce betwixt my flesh and soul.

FREDERIC W. H. MYERS.

FIRST SATURDAY.

Our Lord knew how hard a lesson this virtue was, and He left us no chance for doubting what He commanded, and so escaping its fulfilment. He made His words strong and plain ; He put a reminder of it into our daily prayer, He made our own salvation to hang upon the fulfilment of it. He illustrated it by a parable the most dramatic and forcible. He lived it through all His life, and He died bearing it in His heart and breathing it from His lips. As He lay down on His bed of anguish —"one plank hard and narrow"—and at the moment He experienced the suffering that always harrows one the most to think of—though perhaps not the worst—the nailing of His precious hands upon the wood—we are told that then He said :

"Father, forgive them, for they know not what they do."

O Saviour of the world, by those wounded hands, by those inexplicable tortures, win for us this heavenly grace : obtain for us that we may never, never

(24)

for one moment, endanger our Eternity with Thee, by a thought, a word, an act of unrepented malice. Pray for us—who love Thee—as well as for them who loved Thee not.

If it were not hard there would have been no need to tell us. It is so contrary to our nature; it is perhaps the most distinctive Christian virtue,— the badge of the Children of the Cross. Oh! let us daily search our hearts to see if we are wearing it un- tarnished. To see that there is no hard repellant feeling towards any who may have offended us. " —Would I do them good? Can I pray for them, cheerfully, honestly, not only that they may be brought to repentance, but that they may be blessed, temporally and spiritually? Could I hear without a pang, of their great success and advance- ment? Do I feel that I never want to see them again? If they have repented, could I restore them again to the place which they formerly occupied in my regard?"—For the Prayer says: "forgive us our trespasses as we forgive them that trespass against us." Heaven help us, if it means according to the degree—and that that measure of liberal restitution of favor and love that we show, is to be showed to us. I hope it means,—forgive us,—for we have forgiven. But I fear it does not mean that, and that our love and charity is to be the gauge of our reward The larger, nobler, more loving our forgiveness, the larger, nobler, more loving our Lord's welcome for us. There are degrees of glory. If we just forgive, we may be just saved. Does that content us?

The constant habit of Bishop Boulter to forgive the injuries done to him, led one of his friends to write the following lines after his death, which must be considered the more beautiful, as being true :

"Some write their wrongs in marble, he, more just,
Stoop'd down serene and wrote them in the dust,
Trod under foot, the sport of every wind,
Swept from the earth and blotted from his mind.
There, buried in the dust, he bade them lie,
And grieved they could not 'scape the Almighty's eye!"

SONNET.

We know not how we act, each upon each :—
In the deep Providence of God, on earth
Where strangest mysteries have daily birth
Oft we forget, wounded by hasty speech,
If used aright a power it hath to teach
Humility or meekness else unlearn'd :.

That blessings by such trials may be earn'd,
And we, the heights of holiness may reach.
Hast thou ne'er watch'd a loved one purer grow,
Increase in Faith and Charity and Hope?
The fruit to such, of thine own failings know
Which for the action of each grace gave scope :
And whilst both knelt for sins of deed and tongue
Each, through the other, may have victory won.

———

ANON.

"JESU! Lord.   Who madest me
And with Thy Blood my soul hast bought,
Forgive, if I have grievèd Thee
In word, in will, in deed, in thought.

JESU, in Whom is all my trust,
Who on the tree of scorn didst die,
Withdraw me from all fleshly lust,
From all worldly vanity.

JESU, by the deadly smart
On Thy loving Hands and Feet,
Make me meek and pure in heart
And to love Thee, as is meet.

JESU, by the bitter wound
Open'd in Thy bleeding side,
Let sin, which hath my heart fast bound,
Be wash'd away in that red tide.

JESU CHRIST, on Thee I call ;
Thou art God, and full of might ;
Cleanse me, guard me, lest I fall
In deadly sin, both day and night."

FIRST SUNDAY.

DANIEL, alone and unsupported by outward authority and companionship, fasts three full weeks. The Man clothed in linen, with loins girded with fine gold of Uphaz, says to him these words:

"Fear not, Daniel, for from the first day that thou didst set thine heart to understand, and to chasten thyself before thy God, thy words were heard, and I am come for thy words."

There must be some mysterious virtue in fasting; there must be something that attracts God's favor in self-chastisement. From the first day that Daniel set his heart to understand, and chastened himself before his God, from that day his words were heard. Why must this be? Why does this open the door of Heaven to our words? Why do the angels come for them *then*, and not before? "What I do thou knowest not now, but thou shalt know hereafter." We must be patient about this and be humble. There is nothing that seems more directly against nature than this spiritual law—that we

(28)

should pray best when our miserable bodies are most uncomfortable; that God should hear our words when we are so wearied and so faint that we seem scarcely to hear them ourselves. Fasting does not, cannot, make devotion more comfortable to ourselves, but it can, it does, it seems, make it more acceptable to God. It is easy to understand how doing without food, to give the food to the hungry, might be pleasing to God, and of tangible benefit to some one else. But this does not seem to have been the rule of Daniel's fast—of our Lord's Fast. It simply seems a matter between God and the soul. It is utterly repugnant to human nature, and a mystery; and so it must be taken, and Faith must assume it, for reason cannot. It has something to do with that strange law of suffering—of which the most prominent and most incomprehensible example is the anguish of maternity; the paying for some broken spiritual law by some physical forfeit. God grant us courage always to believe this, if it is the truth, and to abide by it, if it is possible.

"Use thus, my soul, with equal care,
This sad but gracious time;
For prayerless fast, or fastless prayer,
To God shall never climb.

Watch, lest the blessings offer'd thee
　　Through thine own fault be curst,
And thy last state may haply be,
　　Far worse than was thy first."

———

Dear suffering Lord, my Life, my All,
　　My soul is sick with love for Thee,
Break Thou the fetters which enthrall
　　The heart which to Thy breast would flee.

Oh, light the flame of love within
　　Burn out the dross of our dull clay;
That my pure soul absolved from sin
　　In Thine embrace may melt away.

For Thy dear sake let life appear
　　Of small account, of little worth :
For Thy dear sake, with Heaven more near,
　　Take Thou the short lived joys of earth.

When morning calls me from my rest
　　To meet the first beams of the sun,
When evening lingers in the west
　　With silence of the night begun,

In toil, in rest, in work, in sleep,
　　When day begins and ends again,
My faltering footsteps, JESU, keep
　　With Thy protecting love.　Amen.

PHILIP S. WORSLEY.

Through miry paths I labor'd on;
  Dark fell the mist, I could not see;
But when my feet were almost gone,
  A voice said—Turn and look on Me.

Who com'st Thou, taunted like a thief
  By hard men, joyous in Thy fall?
Who art Thou, yearning pale with grief
  To some friend in the Judgment-hall?

O glance, too kind for broken vow,
  For crime sinn'd often and afresh!
O thorns, that wring the purest Brow
  Made ever yet from human flesh!

O printed Hands, O printed Feet,
  O side, dug to the quick with steel!
I marvel, but no answering heat
  Strikes through my breast, to make it feel.

Ah, Lord; but if Thy Grace impart
  True sorrow for my inward stain,
That look will pierce me to the heart,
  That crown will tear me to the brain.

Those marks upon Thy Feet and Hands,
  That furrow in thy sinless Side,
Will tear me as with iron brands
  While I with Thee hang crucified.

Nay, but the World—too far, too much
  She lures me with her power to please.

How can I bear Thy healing touch
    To rob me of my sweet disease?

For even again that path of mire,
    That dim place, where the mist came down,
Seems, for its joy, worth endless fire,
    Such dreams my Soul in poison drown.

I bathe me in a false delight,
    Chew dust for bread: yet, Lord, I pray,
Come, for without Thee day is night,
    Come now, for with Thee night is day.

Yea, by Thy Love, Thy Toil to save,
    Thy Prayer, Thy Groans, Thy bloody Sweat,
Thy Death, Thy Rising from the Grave,
    Look down from Heaven, and hear me yet.
                    GERALD MOULTRIE.

FIRST MONDAY.

IF anything could frighten a careless, easy, every-day Christian, one would think it would be the reading of the 3d of St. James. And it is so awfully practical, so true on its very face, so searchingly direct, like all of St. James. It is impossible to get away from it: we know these are the words of a man who is a master of human motives and experiences. This fire of hell, this world of iniquity, this unruly evil, this deadly poison—this Tongue is the possession, is the plague, is the constant, close, clinging companion of every one of us. None exempt; in our little way or our great way, we are daily, hourly sowing evil—blessing God vainly, cursing man foully. This devil is our inheritance ; this perhaps comes not out but by prayer and fasting. This concerns us all. There is nothing for it but watching, praying, praying, watching—from childhood to old age.

Who sins not in this member in man's sight? Think of all the multitudes with whom we have conversed, in all our lives. Out of them all; perhaps of two or three, we remember, we have never heard them utter an unkind, harsh, or hasty word. Think of it; with our blunted perceptions, our dull ears, even we have felt the air to be full of fatal, foul, ungrateful, flippant words. How must the clamor sound in the ears of Infinite Purity? How can He be so long patient?

And how shall we take heed unto our ways that we offend not in our tongue? That we plant not evil in the hearts of men; that we pain not the ear of our patient God; that we send not out our evil thoughts as devils to do the devil's work; that we glorify God in our body and in our spirit, which are His? Great God! we know not, teach us. It is so incessant, so unremitting a warfare, we tremble when we think of it; but give us courage and make us to pray incessantly. "Set a watch, O Lord, upon my mouth, and keep the door of my lips." When we think of the frightful multitude of these evils, which every day of our lives we have committed, and that it is only of the grosser ones of which we have repented, and of which we ever knew, should we not be filled with fright and shame. The strictness of the watch which must be

kept, the purification of the sight which is required to know the sins which are swarming from
our lips; how can we attain unto it! Lord, do
Thou teach us.

"Unadvisedly with his lips."

"Over the cedars beyond Jordan growing,
Come, balmy breeze! and touch the old man's cheek,
Come from the land with milk and honey flowing;
His eyes not dim, his natural strength not weak,
He stands and gazes from Abarim's peak,
But never shall his weary foot pass o'er
Like a glad bird to that desirèd shore.

Sweet as the image fair in every part
The mother pictures of her babe unborn,
Feeling the burden at her happy heart;
Dear as his home to wayfarer forlorn;
As to the youth his hope of bridal morn;
So dear, so sweet had been that old man's dream
Of the good land beyond the silver stream.

How oft, when Pharaoh's halls were wild with joy
That vision like a strain of music stole
O'er the long musings of the Hebrew boy.
How often, like a charm, it used to roll
Before him in the desert when his soul
Was weary, and his spirit fail'd within,
Vex'd with the people's selfishness and sin.

And now it lies before him, all embalm'd,
In odors like a garden; and he stands
Like a good ship just in the port becalm'd—
Her crew hang o'er her sides with idle hands,
And all their wives and daughters throng the sands,
Gaze on the outstretch'd arms they cannot reach,
And hear their voices murmur from the beach.

There lies the golden end of all his hopes,
To fancy fair, more beautiful to sight;
The blue-topp'd mountains with long sunny slopes,
And deep green hollows bathed in purple light;
The foam-white streamlets leaping from the height,
And stretching far away the chequer'd plain,
Red with its grape, and yellow with its grain.

But he may never cross the silver river,
Because in Kadesh, where the people strove,
He sinn'd to the Lord God; and so forever
He turns from the fond dream his childhood wove,
His boyhood's eager hope, his manhood's love—
Turns with quick quivering lip and streaming eye,
And lies down on the mountain top to die.

Come, sinful soul, where purple Pisgah dips
Her brow in clouds; watch by this dying Saint,
Once spake he unadvisedly with his lips,
Are not thine full of anger and complaint,
Words quick and light, or with a fouler taint?
He *once* rebell'd—then what of thee whose life
Is one long treason, one continual strife?

And, O for him, though life's dear hope was blighted,
Better that mountain grave by hands undrest,
Where soft winds sang, and angel forms alighted;
For sweeter far than Israel's promised rest
Forever safe to lie down with the blest,
And fairer still than Canaan's boasted sod
Th' eternal hills, the Paradise of God."

CECIL FRANCES ALEXANDER.

FIRST TUESDAY.

This people honoreth me with their lips—but their heart is far from me.—St. Mark vii. 6.

The Pharisees and certain of the Scribes "which came from Jerusalem" and undoubtedly were full of authority, and of great weight among the people, came to our Lord, as usual, to find fault. The disciples had eaten bread with unwashen hands. Then our Lord finds fault with *them*, condemning them in their own prophet's words. (vs. 6 and 7.)

But indeed He did not condemn a Jewish fault alone: it is a human fault, a fault deep planted in our nature. It is, to grasp the present, the visible, and let go the intangible, the invisible. It is so hard to live for an idea, to eat and drink with reference to Heaven fifty years hence, and not with reference to our little rule which we have made for ourselves. We set up our little laws and they become our gods; and are to us instead of mercy, goodness and truth. What a state of grace that would be to reach, when the great Spiritual laws

(38)

would be as present to the mind, as tenaciously clung to as the little rules which every Christian makes for himself or receives from those that guide him. Not but that the little laws are good; and it is true no doubt that God remembers the Spirit in which we began them, the intention then, and not the mechanical performance now.

But, oh! to live above the narrow day which we can see. Surely natures of old must have been freer and less bound to sight than ours are, or there would have been no saints. How is it possible that saints could have had the trial that we have! Whatever we touch turns to clay. If we have a grand aspiration we put it into a resolution, and in a moment it is material, it is connected with earth, it is dull, and has lost its heavenliness. If we can put a duty into prose, it is done. "The world is too much with us." We cannot free ourselves. We long to translate everything into fact, and then make ourselves machines and carry out the task we have set ourselves. The duties we cannot do with our hands, or our feet, or our tongues, oh! those are the duties that the God who is a Spirit values.

"O God! while I strive to serve Thee with the body Thou has given me, do Thou purify—exalt—

feed—lighten—the Spirit which I so neglect. It is
Thine—the body is my bondage, the soul is Thine,
by right of law, and by gift and will of mine. Forget, my God, the dull acts; remember what I meant
when first I said the prayer, resolved the fast, sacri-
ficed the pleasure. Put life into my dull death, and
love me now and ever."

———

LORD! I am Thine, Thy little child;
Though fiercely still within, and wild
 The fires of youth may burn;
Oh be not angry if I weep,
And dread these stormy waters deep—
 Master! to Thee I turn.

And, if in zeal and forward haste,
All rashly from the ship I pass'd,
 And tempted danger here,
Too great for one so weak as me,
Yet LORD, it was to come to Thee;
 Oh let me find Thee near!

Nor in these days of dimness holy
And Spirit-searching melancholy,
 Strengthen my drooping heart:
And let me stop each wayward sense
In pure and secret abstinence,
 And from the world depart.

The Church my Mother, calls me on
To follow JESUS, all alone
   Across the desert lea;
And wrestle with the Tempter there
In vigils of incessant prayer
   And with wild beasts to be.

And well I know, when weak and faint
With weary days in fasting spent,
   I must lose sight of Him;
And peevish thoughts and tempers ill
The ardor of my breast will chill,
   And make my lamp burn dim.

Then by the hour that saw me rest
Safe as a fledgling in his nest,
   Within the white robe's fold;
And by the cross that on my brow
He signed—the seal that devils know—
   JESUS! Thy son uphold!

But I will quell my doubts and fears,
And on where holy Sinai rears
   Its form before my eyes;
For I can see above its head
A rim of growing glory spread,
   The light of Easter skies!

                F. W. FABER.

SECOND WEDNESDAY.

———◆———

Then shall all tribes of the earth mourn.—St. Matthew xxiv.

THE day that cometh not with observation; that lightens upon us in an instant; that breaks up night and sleep; that throws down all the laws of nature and of life; that flames upon the heavens the Sign of the Son of Man; that darts through every intellect and every conscience in the universe at the same moment the same thought; that rouses to instant and sudden consciousness millions and millions of dead men and women; that paralyzes with sharp and sudden awe millions and millions of living men and women; this is the day of which the Evangelist says, "And then shall all the tribes of the earth mourn."

But why should they mourn, who are bidden to look up, and lift up their heads when their redemption draweth nigh? Why should they mourn, who have been patiently waiting for Christ through years of discipline? Who have learned to say, "Come, Lord JESUS," knowing that their prayer might be the prayer for which He waited; who have yearned to look upon His face, even by the light of the Day of Doom; who have watched for Him as they that watch for the morning.

Ah! they are not of the tribes of the earth. They are of the house and lineage of their Lord. The sign of the Son of Man is in their foreheads and on their breasts. There are two great tribes now on the earth: those who serve God in their souls and in their bodies, and those who serve Him not, and have no better rule for their souls and bodies than the instincts of pleasure, or the dictates of reason. Those who *worship* Him; those upon whose bodies, as well as souls, His mark has been placed; those who have acknowledged His Spiritual Kingdom and made haste into it; those who have worn away by fast and prayer some of their fleshly nature; those who have believed and put into words their faith; who have professed Him before men, who have, even in the humblest and most modest fashion, exerted themselves to work the works that pleased Him, and have not pleased themselves; those who, with a million imperfections, have yet the germ of spiritual life in their natures; oh! for them the Day of the Lord will not bring mourning.

The tribes of the Earth. What is it to be of them? To be easy and happy and bountiful; to be contented with things as they are; to love Nature; to love one's own; to think with rapture of the beautiful; to pay God no tangible service; to call all worship of Him superstition, that is not intellectual; to be selfish and self-surrounded, and self-satisfied, even though possessed of gentleness and lovely attributes. This is to be of the tribes of the Earth. To be morose, hard, pitiless. To be sensual, pleasure-loving, unthinking. To be bold, defiant, mocking. To be indolent, languid, inattentive. To refuse Him worship, to disregard His plain commands, to give Him our body's service and deny Him our soul's allegiance, or to give Him spiritual homage and resent His claim upon our mortal powers; this is to be of those that mourn in that Day.

Oft shall that flesh imperil and outweary
    soul that would stay it in the straiter scope,
oft shall the chill day and the even dreary
    force on my heart the frenzy of a hope.

lo ! as some ship, outworn and overladen,
    strains for the harbor where her sails are furl'd;
lo ! as some innocent and eager maiden
    leans o'er the wistful limit of the world,

dreams of the glow and glory of the distance,
  wonderful wooing and the grace of tears,
dreams with what eyes and what a sweet insistance,
  lovers are waiting in the hidden years :—

lo ! as some venture, from his stars receiving,
  promise and presage of sublime emprise,
wears evermore the seal of his believing
  deep in the dark of solitary eyes,

yea, to the end, in palace or in prison,
  fashions his fancies of the realm to be,
fallen from the height or from the deeps arisen,
  ring'd with the rocks and sunder'd of the sea :

so even I, and with a heart more burning,
  so even I, and with a hope more sweet,
groan for the hour, O Christ ! of Thy returning,
  faint for the flaming of Thine advent feet.

                    FREDERIC W. H. MYERS.

Almighty Judge, how shall poor wretches brook
      Thy dreadful look,
Able a heart of iron to appall,
      When Thou shalt call
    For every man's peculiar book ?

What others mean to do, I know not well;
    Yet I hear tell,
That some will turn Thee to some leaves therein
    So void of sin
That they in merit shall excell.

But I resolve, when Thou shall call for mine,
    That to decline,
And thrust a Testament into Thy hand:
    Let that be scann'd,
There Thou shalt find my faults are Thine.

GEORGE HERBERT.

SECOND THURSDAY.

TRULY we stand in the ranks of a great army that nightly lies down to rest without any certain knowledge of the march or battle that is to be to-morrow. We come up in a great wall of human energy and movement—but we pause; there is not one of all the millions who can say, what the next day has for him or them—what the next hour holds in its mysterious grasp. The brains, the wills, the tongues; what do they all accomplish as far as this thing goes? The wisest philosopher on earth cannot tell what faces will meet him on the street to-morrow, what sky will cover him, what sensations of pleasure or of pain, what physical or mental changes may pass over him; he is not much better than the baby in the nursery for all that. He does not know whether his soul will be in his body twelve hours from now; and all the science, all the philosophy of all the ages, cannot help him to the knowledge. Should not that make us very humble? What are we that we should demand to understand before we accept—to see before we assent. Truly each day's combination of events and sensations is a mystery that we cannot refuse because we have not seen it, because we could not predict it. We have to take so much from God, our coming into, our going out of life, our breath, our brain, our relations to Him as our Creator; why cannot we humbly take His mandates, His revelations (beyond which mystery stands beyond mystery) concerning spiritual things. I should think the spirit that demands a sign, must be destestable to God. A thousand times He says, *Only believe.* And what else can we do but believe. Many turn back and walk no more with Him for some "hard saying." If they had gone forward, they would have found it a saying perhaps which though still hard to the mind, was clear and transparent to the soul. "The heart hath its reasons which the reason cannot comprehend."

We know not what a day may bring forth; His mercies are new every morning; let each day be consecrated by an act of trust; let us take our lives by this boundary which He has marked in so many ways. Let our cares be limited to a day's length, our prayers most practical and earnest for the day on which we are entering. Let us have faith in the small practical matters of every day as well as in the great mysteries of the spiritual and eternal life.

LENT.

I.

Yes! I have walk'd the world these two months past
With quick free step, loud voice, and youth's slight cheer;
And dull and weary were the shadows cast
From the dark cross and Lent's dim portals near.

II.

Yes! I rode up with such a noisy state
And retinue of all things bright and fair,
And reach'd in this new pilgrim guise the gate,
As though my dreams might have free passage there.

III.

Dreams of far travel, visionary love,
Hopes, memories, sweet songs, and sunny faces,
Cheering each other on, with me did move
Some way on Lent's keen roads and desert places.

IV.

And many a pilgrim wending o'er the plain,
With face half-veil'd and tear-drops flowing fast,
Marvell'd perchance at that unsightly train,
When I and my strange servitors rode past.

4

V.

But every stone that lay along the way,
Wounding the feet of those who travell'd by,
Each sleety shower, chill blast, and cloudy day,
Scatter'd my poor soft-living company.

VI.

Thus as my spirit more and more drank in
The deep mysterious dimness of the time,
Old forms waxed pale, and lines and shapes of sin
Wore hardly off, and my baptismal prime

VII.

Grew into color and distinctness there;
But my blythe train and equipage were gone,
The songs and sunny smiles; my heart was bare,
With Lent all darkening round me, and alone.

VIII.

O joy of all our joys! to be bereft
Of our false power to make the world so dear!
O joy of all our joys! to be thus left
In our wild years, with none but Jesus near.

IX.

How sweetly then shall Lent's few Sundays shock
The sadness which itself hath now grown sweet,
Like the soft striking of an old church clock,
Making the heart of summer midnight beat.

X.

How sweetly now shall this most Holy gloom
Gather and double on my chasten'd heart,
Circling with dark bright folds the Garden-Tomb,
Where Lent and I, like Christian friends, shall part.

F. W. FABER.

SECOND FRIDAY.

Come unto me all ye that travail and are heavy laden, and I will refresh you.—St. Matthew xi. 28.

The Saviour stands with gracious outstretched hands of invitation. To every one is His word of comfort spoken. For who is not burdened? We are so used to our burdens that we never fully realize them. Look upon the face of the dead, ten minutes after the dire struggle of dissolution. Already the peaceful look that has been unfamiliar to it in life, has smoothed away its contractions, relaxed its habitual and painful tensions, and there is, perhaps, the expression that you have never seen since childhood, though you have looked upon the features daily.

Our faces, our bodies are worn with the pressure of our heavy lading; never, till we have laid it down, does it appear what we have carried. Think how much we make our lives ourselves; think how our lives bring our discipline; think of the constant struggle between flesh and spirit; the strange move-

(52)

ments and unknown sphere of the mind, the un-
accounted effects of the body upon it; are they
not both burdened, do they not groan and travail together in pain, being burdened? This, irrespective
of special afflictions, extraordinary chastisements,
sorrows for which the world pities our condition.
And what remedy does the Man of Sorrows offer to
us, seeing our state? The first part of our cure
must be a sense of our burden. The indifferent, the
stolid, the careless, cannot be the subjects of this
healing. Then faith, to go to Him, instead of those
who offer us assistance here. Acceptance of His service, submission to His rule, obedience to His outer
and inner laws. And we are helped. It is strange.
We know not how. It is laying down an intangible
burden, and taking up a tangible one. But it is a
magic change. Look at the face of the man or the
woman who has, more markedly than others, come
out from the world, and separated himself or herself
from its pleasures, its toils, its rules. Those who
depart not from the temple, but serve Him with
fastings and prayers. Those who follow Him to
prison and to death; those who turn their faces from
the bright places of the earth and seek the dimmest,
for love to Him, and to His little ones. What do

these faces tell us? Oh! let us learn the lesson well.
There is no mistaking it. So far as we follow their
example, so far shall we find refreshment. The lesson is so old, so plain, so trite, we half of us are
missing it. Sell all thou hast; this peace is worth
it. The burden is greater than thou canst bear.
Why not get rid of it? There is a way—a way we
have known since we were old enough to understand.
How strange we do not come! O Lord, be patient
yet a little longer!

—

Mortal! if e'er thy spirit faint,
 By grief or pain oppresst,
Seek not vain hope, or sour complaint,
 To cheer or ease thy breast;

But view thy bitterest pangs as sent
 A shadow of that doom,
Which is the soul's just punishment
 In its own guilt's true home.

Be thine own judge; hate thy proud heart;
 And while the sad drops flow,
E'en let thy will attend the smart,
 And sanctify thy woe.

JOHN HENRY NEWMAN.

Oh, at the foot of it
  Let me lie down!
Clasp it, and cling to it,
  More than a crown!

Wrapt in my penitence,
  Muffled with shame;
Shelter'd from honor,
  Rescued from fame.

O all my agony,
  Let but one eye;
Only one merciful
  Saviour, descry!

Only one hand on
  The stricken to strike;
He who was tempted
  And stricken alike.

There with its sorceries
  Sin cannot come;
There with its flatteries
  Falsehood is dumb;

There grief is sanctity,
  Pain cannot wring;
Sin hath no pleasure,
  Death hath no sting.

Sceptres and empires,
  Worlds, are but dross,
Lord! when I lay me down
  Clasping Thy cross.
             ANON.

Silence in heaven and earth!
    The hush of love or fear!
His voice the Highest sendeth forth;
    The still small voice is here.
The world's hoarse murmurs under,
    Its loudest din above,
It speaketh not in thunder,
    But in words, and the tone is love.
It calls, and a gift it offers;
    To whom are those words address'd?
"Come, *ye that are heavy laden*,
    And I will give you *rest.*"

Ye that have toil'd in vain,
    Till strength and hope have fled,
And lavish'd the years that come not again,
    For that which is not bread;
Ye who are toiling now,
    Weary in heart and limb,
With a strength each day more low,
    And a hope each day more dim;
Weary in soul and spirit
    Toiling with hearts oppress'd,
"Come to me, all that labor,
    And I will give you rest."

Is guilt unpardon'd there
    With heavy hand and strong,
The weight in the air of measureless fear,
    Or of hope deferred long?
The sorrow which freezeth tears

With the force of a sudden blow,
The long, dull pressure of weary years,
   Bowing you silently low?
Many the burdens and hard
   Wherewith the heart is press'd:
"Come *all* that are *heavy* laden
   And I will give you rest."

The world has many a promise
   To beguile the blithe and young;
But to you the world is honest,
   It has ceased to promise long.
Wealth, pleasures, fame, successes,
   The world has store of these;
For you no cure it professes,
   It offers you no ease.
But Christ has an arm almighty,
   And a balm for the faintest breast;
"Come, ye that are heavy laden,
   And I will give you rest."

Would ye fain, among the sleepers,
   In dust your tired hearts bow?
The rest He gives is deeper,
   And He will give it *now*.
No dull, oblivious sleep
   In the lull of pain repress'd,
But all your hearts to sleep
   In perfect and conscious rest;
Rest that shall make you strong
   To serve among the bless'd.

" Come, all ye that are heavy laden,
  And I will give you rest."

The rest of a happy child,
  Led by the Father on,
Feeling His smile, and reconciled
  To all that He has done;
Of one who can meekly bend
  Neath the yoke of the Lord who died;
Of a soldier who knows how the fight will end
  With a Leader true and tried;
The rest of a subject heart,
  Of its best desires possess'd.
" Come, ye that are heavy laden,
  And I will give you rest."

Rest from sin's crushing debt,
  In the blood which Christ has shed;
From the pang of vain regret,
  In the thought that He has led.
Rest in His perfect love;
  Rest in His tender care;
Rest in His presence for you above,
  In his presence with you here.
Rest in Him slain and risen,
  The Lamb, and the Royal Priest.
" Come, all that are heavy laden,
  And I will give you rest."

                                    MRS. CHARLES.

SECOND SATURDAY.

ANXIETY OF MIND.

SOME one says, anxiety is the worst of all evils except sin. It certainly hides God's face from us, and it is our own hand that draws the veil. For anxiety is directly contrary to the Commandment. Is it spiritually for ourselves? Cast all your care upon Him. Is it for our brethren spiritually? It cost more to redeem their souls—so we must let that alone forever. Is it for temporal matters? Take no thought for the morrow. Your Lord knoweth of what you have need—your Lord who holds all gifts in His hand, and all sympathy in His heart. You have permission to tell Him, but there let it end. Leave your petition at the foot of His throne and go away with a calm soul.

But how, when our nerves are unstrung—when cares like autumn leaves strew our path, and every step recalls the fact that they are there; when our hearts are heavy with apprehensions which are almost realities; when our days are full of petty, fretting

(59)

duties, and our nights are weary to unconsciousness; when all our hours are blotted and blurred with irregular demands upon our time; when there seems no calm surface in our hearts, which can reflect the brooding Dove of Peace; when we hate the turmoil, and long for the peace which we can less than ever understand; *How* can we but be anxious and troubled about many things?

How? How do Martyrs bear the flame, the sword? There must be a way. These are our scorching, picking, goading torments. And there must be a way to bear them to God's glory. May be we are bearing some which we need not bear. "Make straight paths for your feet." Judge and arrange between your conscience and your temptations, and then courageously discard the superfluous, and deal with the others on your knees. Pray passionately for calm, and for a collected spirit; think about it incessantly; think about great things, and try to realize the insignificance of some of the things that trouble you, and turn your mind from the sins of others. Trust God; and keep trusting him, and remind yourself to trust Him.

Said an ancient hermit, bending
   Half in prayer upon his knee,
"Oil I need for midnight watching
   I desire an olive-tree."

Then he took a tender sapling,
   Planted it before his cave,
Spread his trembling hands above it,
   As his benison he gave.

But he thought, the rain it needeth,
   That the root may drink and swell:
"God! I pray Thee send Thy showers!"
   So a gentle shower fell.

"Lord! I ask for beams of summer,
   Cherishing this little child."
Then the dripping clouds divided,
   And the sun look'd down and smiled.

"Send it frost to brace its tissues,'
   O my God!" the hermit cried.
Then the plant was bright'and hoary,
   But at evensong it died.

Went the hermit to a brother
   Sitting in his rocky cell:
"Thou an olive-tree possesseth;
   How is this, my brother, tell?

"I have planted one, and pray'd,
   Now for sunshine, now for rain;
God hath granted each petition,
   Yet my olive-tree hath slain!"

Said the other, "I entrusted
    To its God my little tree;
He who made knew what it needed
    Better than a man like me.

"Laid I on Him no condition,
    Fix'd not ways and means; so I
Wonder not my olive thriveth,
    Whilst thy olive-tree did die."

S. BARING-GOULD.

———

"Fret not, poor soul, while doubt and fear
    Disturb thy breast;
The pitying Angels who can see
How vain thy wild regret must be,
    Say—Trust and Rest.

Plan not, nor scheme—but calmly wait;
    His choice is best:
While blind and erring is thy sight
His wisdom sees and judges right,
    So—Trust and Rest.

Strive not nor struggle: thy poor might
    Can never wrest,
The meanest thing to serve thy will;
All power is His alone: be still
    And Trust and Rest.

Desire not: self-love is strong
    Within thy breast;
· And yet He loves thee better still
So let Him do His loving will
    And Trust and Rest.

What dost thou fear? His Wisdom reigns
    Supreme confess'd:
His power is infinite; His love
Thy deepest, fondest dreams above—
    So, Trust and Rest."

Only the present is thy part and fee,
    And happy thou,
If, though thou didst not beat thy future brow,
    Thou couldst well see
What present things required of thee.

They ask enough: why shouldst thou further go?
    Raise not the mud
Of future depths, but drink the clear and good.
    Dig not for woe
In times to come; for it will grow.

Man and the present fit: if he provide,
    He breaks the square,
This hour is mine: if for the next I care,
    I grow too wide,
And do encroach upon death's side.

God claims the dog till night; wilt loose the chain,
    And wake thy sorrow?
Wilt thou forestall it, and now grieve to-morrow,
    And then again
  Grieve over freshly all thy pain?

Either grief will not come; or if it must,
    Do not forecast:
And while it cometh, it is almost past.
    Away distrust:
  My God hath promised; He is just.

GEORGE HERBERT.

SECOND SUNDAY.

For this is the will of God, even your Sanctification.—I THESS. iv. 3.

THIS is the message of God to every one that reads it, that hears it. God wills our sanctification —our making ourselves pure, our making ourselves clean—putting away what offends, and making ourselves fit for His use—for holy service. The temples of the Holy Ghost: mysterious honor. How can we dare to make these temples what they are; how can we dare to disregard the words, and not think of·them at all. Surely we need the whole power of the Godhead to fight against the sins of impurity, even the very smallest. For there is nothing that so kills the soul, that so takes the very core out of our faith, as this. It deadens our conscience, it blinds our eyes, it turns that which before had been a mystery into flat nothingness. High things are no more, to the mind that admits evil. God Him-

5   (65)

self ceases to exist in the faith of such a one, at least in everything but name. What a change passes over the spiritual life! Is this the same heart that prayed, that aspired, that saw visions? How light, how low, how flippant are the thoughts that fill it now! There are a great many temptations, which if yielded to a little, still leave us with the will to turn to God. This temptation, if yielded to in ever so slight a degree, leaves us without any attraction towards Him; cold, dead, dull, everything heaven-ly looks now. We have a long road to go back again before we can see Him as we saw Him before we sinned. The pure in heart shall see God. That is the very actual fact. And the impure cannot see Him. What an awful thought: to be blind, while we apprehend no danger. Where may we not be going, what horror, what pitfall may we not be near? What end may we not be reaching? Even eternal loss, and yet feeling not, seeing not.—

> "Seal but thine eyes to pleasant things,
>   Love's glorious world will on thee burst."

O who would not see! Both worlds at once. The fairness and true beauty of this, and the glory, the magnificence of that! Can any effort be too rigorous to purge our mental view from the mists of fleshly lusts. But how? First, prayer. No one can be so pure they do not need to pray for purity. Prayer against all temptation, against this temptation in particular. Closing up the avenues that lead to it; and they are, vanity and self-indulgence.

Vanity is the foolish little half-reproved portress, who throws open the door for a dark masked sin to enter the heart, a heart that may have been so innocent and so childish, no word of caution had ever been spoken to it.

And self-indulgence, how many will confess it was through this path the tempter came. A life easy, undisciplined; promising and intending good, but not in effect at all self-denying. A life in its practical interpretation not differing from worldly lives, only consecrated by a spiritual, theoretical affinity with good, an inner consciousness of purity, a love of the beautiful, an attraction towards the true. Ah! what wild work does temptation make in such a heart. How theories are scattered, how idols fall prone! How every good thing is turned to evil! The sin becomes the true, the good, the beautiful. It is a long, long way back, that soul has to go to be ready to begin to see God again, or approach the outer gates of His refulgent splendor.

This is a practical, simple way of walking near to God, of keeping out of great sins, of gradually effecting the work of "sanctification." But it is so simple, impatient souls rebel, and would rather some great thing were ordered for their cure. It is an actual every-day service of God; praying to Him, going to church, reading good books even when they are irksome; practising self-denials even when they seem to have no end, but are simply done to assert our sense of our own desert of punishment. A continual effort to be humble; a constant attempt to realize our Baptismal separation from the world around us. Little, practical, every-day discipline, that seems to have no relation to the great crises of life, that seems only fit for children. How is that to prepare us for the great temptations, the breaking, crushing passes through which our paths may lie? How do years of even life, attention to the laws of health, making the best of physical strength, keeping practically before one the rules our intelligence has recognized, fit one to go through a long attack of illness? "Every thing is in his favor, he has led such a regular life." And yet he did not think much about the fever when he went through these daily dictates of good sense. He was only doing what seemed right, and was unconsciously preparing himself for the great ordeal through which years hence he was to pass. So it is with our soul's sanctification. It is hard to see how these little practical details will effect us in the great, and perhaps sudden, attacks of the Evil One ; how they will prepare us for all the hard days which we know must come, and which we scarcely dare dwell upon in fancy. For life, for death, we must sanctify ourselves by means that seem beneath the occasion that we are to meet. The secret of all is faith and submission.

———

We have two things to do, to live and die:
To win another and a longer life
Out of this earthly change and weary strife ;
That catch the hours that one by one go by,
And write the Cross upon them as they fly.
So shall they lay their burden gently down,
Sinking, perchance hard-by, beneath the Throne,
Withdrawn anew into eternity.
'Tis hard to live by youth's fast bubbling springs
And treat our loves, joys, hopes, as flowery things

That for awhile may climb the boughs, and twine
Among the prickly leaves of discipline.
Yet, wouldst thou rise in Christ's self-mastering school,
Thy very heart itself must beat by rule.

F. W. FABER.

———

"MULTUM DILEXIT."

She sat and wept beside His feet; the weight
Of sin oppress'd her heart; for all the blame
And the poor malice of the worldly shame
To her was past, extinct and out of date,
Only the *sin* remain'd—the leprous state;
She would be melted by the heat of love—
By fires far fiercer than are blown to prove
And purge the silver ore adulterate.
She sat and wept, and with her untress'd hair
Still wiped the Feet she was so blest to touch;
And He wiped off the soiling of despair
From her sweet soul, because she loved so much;
I am a sinner, full of doubts and fears
Make me an humble thing of love and tears.

HARTLEY COLERIDGE.

SECOND MONDAY.

The Calling of St. Peter.—ST. MATTHEW iv. 18.

THE story of this event differs in the four Gospels; though it is related in all. First St. Matthew tells it in three verses; how Christ was walking by the sea of Galilee and saw the two brothers at work with their nets; and calling them and promising them to be "fishers of men," is straitway obeyed, and they leave all and follow Him. Then follows, equally concisely, the calling of the two sons of Zebedee.

In St. Mark's Gospel, the narrative is almost precisely the same. St. Luke gives a different version; but undoubtedly they can all be harmonized. It is a longer account, beginning with the use of St. Peter's ship by our Lord, who from it preached to the people, crowding about Him on the shore. Then after His sermon is ended, He turns to St. Peter and directs him to launch out into the deep and let down his net. Then follows the miraculous draught of fishes; the calling by Simon and Andrew of their partners, the sons of Zebedee; the conver-

(71)

sion and astonishment of all these; the assurance
"Fear not, from henceforth thou shalt catch men."
And their forsaking all and following Him.

In St. John's Gospel, it is Andrew (who, having
joined in the train of John the Baptist's disciples
who had followed Christ to His abode, had heard
Him and been convinced), takes his brother Simon to
the Saviour, assuring him that he has found the
Messiah. And Jesus, beholding him, gives to him
his name of Cephas. Nothing is said here of the
two brothers James and John.

All but St. John say strongly, they forsook all
and followed Him. St. Matthew and St. Mark say
they did it "straitway." St. Luke says "they brought
their ships to land" and forsook all and followed
Him. There seems indeed to have been no lagging,
no doubting, no parleying. It seems very easy to
us now to have left all, and been made majestic
princes and apostles, fathers and founders of the
Kingdom of God on Earth. But it would perhaps
have looked very differently to us, on that day, by
the shore of Galilee. The leaving promptly, instantly
the ship, for which, undoubtedly, they had worked
hard in storm and shine. The giving up the occupation of their lives, the routine into which they

had settled; how little details would have rushed
into their minds : that debt outstanding, that sum
of money owing them, the leak that if not attended
to at once might make the boat worthless in a little
time; the nets, unwashed and torn if left lying on
the shore in this condition, would prove a total loss.
What would their neighbors say; what would those
at home advise. How could they come back and
resume their occupation, if this strange prophet had
deceived them? Life was much the same then as
now. Human nature quite the same. It must
have required high faith to leave all and follow
Christ in those days; to leave all straitway; to
leave one's pelf at the mercy of the passers-by; to
fix upon one's self forever the name and character of
a total stranger. I am afraid there are whole
churches full of Christians who would fail if that
test could be tried upon their faith. How many of
us *now* forsake, not all, but the part He indicates,
for Him? How many of us are living a life of devotion and self-sacrifice? How many of us are giving up what we think *doubtful things* for the sake
of being with Him through eternity. How many
have broken away from conventionalities and have
dedicated themselves to holiness in *any* way which

in which He might lead them ? How many more have, in their hearts, acknowledged Him, but have lingered yet awhile to stop the leak, to mend the net, to take counsel of the world, to adjust and prepare the things of time, before they gave in their adhesion to the Sovereign of Eternity. This must seem cold and small to Him who loved not His life unto the death. He may still care to save such ; but He cannot love them as He loves those who follow Him " straitway," who leave *all* to follow Him.

Let it be our resolution to be ready always for any sacrifice, little or great, that may come up as our duty. To court sacrifice, as being sure it cannot harm us, and may please Him. To look always on life as being very inferior to duty. To govern our opinion of the importance of things by a recollection of their *temporalness* or *eternalness.*

Awake, my soul ! and for the strife
Of onward, upward Christian life
 In earnest faith prepare ;
Where the fight rages, fierce and high,
Goes forth the Church's chivalry
 And thou too must be there.

Thy Lord awaits thee in the field,
Bring forth the spear, essay the shield
   And bind thine armor on;
Low though thou art, for thee there's fame,
By thee a high and honor'd name
   And glory may be won.

Never, in tourney or in fight
Did warrior old win name so bright,
   As thou mayst win and wear,
If like the valiant ones of old
Thy faith be high, thy heart be bold
   To do, as well as dare.

Not with a sword by bloodshed stain'd,
Not for a wreath, that, soon as gain'd,
   Shall fade upon thy brow;
But with the sword of God's good word,
And for the " well done " of thy Lord
   Go forth and conquer now.

Wait not till foes in serried line
And burnish'd armor flash and shine
   To tempt thee to the fray;
Thine enemies are all around
And every spot is battle ground
   Where thou canst watch and pray.

In little things of common life,
There lies the Christian's noblest strife

When he does conscience make
Of every thought and throb within
And words and looks of self and sin
   Crushes for JESU'S sake.

And all the while no glory sees
Save in his own infirmities,
   Which magnify the grace
That out of weakness strength can bring
And give so low and vile a thing
   In God's high work a place.

Then up, my soul, and onward press
To JESUS, in the wilderness
   He waits and fights for thee ;
Thy love to Him devoutly prove
By deeds, not words, and let His love
   Thy shield and buckler be.

                              J. S. B. MONSELL.

SECOND TUESDAY.

Opus quale sit ignis probabit.

A RECAPITULATION of the simplest and most evident of the Christian's duty to his neighbor, and then the Apostle preaches his Advent Sermon. It is high time to awake out of sleep, for now is our salvation nearer than when we believed. The night is far spent; the day is at hand. In view of this, arouse you, be men, do your work and make ready for the Day of God. Hundreds of years ago that sermon was preached to those who had come into the Kingdom or hesitated to come. Millions of souls, passing out of life daily in those hundreds of years, have believed that the day was at hand, for the world as well as for themselves; have laid themselves down to die with the strong belief that though they were not to see the dawning of the day of wrath, the day of wrath was coming while yet their children lived. The days are very evil, the times are waxing late. It is very strange, that belief in the nearness of Christ's coming, that so many

(77)

Christian souls have had. And still He has not come. It is very trite to say, but it is all we can say, for them the times were waxing late, and their day of doom was come; the end of time. What is time—what is it to have it cease? What is it to be a spirit and to have a spirit's life? To count no more by days and hours? To have it with us perhaps as with the Lord, a thousand years as one day, and one day as a thousand years? What does it mean to have it so? How will it feel—what will be the gauge of existence when mortality is past? Will it be emotions; will it be the strength and vitality of our spirituality? Certainly it will *not* be anything that we have learned here. All that is to be put off, the knowledge, the aspirations, the affections of time, in which spirituality has no part. *Opus quale sit ignis probabit.* Let us build wisely! Since the fire is to pass over all, let us impregnate with thoughts and purposes of holiness the least and commonest of our works. We cannot build with ether, and with melody. We must build with clay, because we are working on the earth. But let us render safe against that day each brick we lay, by prayer, by holy intention, by recollectedness of mind. So shall it stand when the elements shall melt with fervent heat. Horrible day of fire! When all shall seem passing away from us, and the heavens are on fire and are dissolving ! When nothing is left to us, nothing, but the spiritual life of our souls. The love which we have borne and do bear to Christ, the sanctification of those forgotten deeds and prayers, which are all that live in God's sight, all that count in the Eternal Kingdom. O frightful folly and sin! Why must we cling about our sordid pleasures, and our anxious cares and hear not Him that speaketh from Heaven. Soberly, reasonably, and with a holy purpose, why cannot we begin our immortality here, and strengthen ourselves to appear on the day when mortality shall wither and scorch before the first breath of that awful flame.

Great God! what manner of persons ought we to be in all holy conversation and godliness!

———

Hark, a joyful voice is thrilling,
  And eac'ı dim and winding way
Of the ancient Temple filling;
  Dreams, depart! for it is day.

Christ is coming! from thy bed
  Earth-bound soul, awake and spring,

With the sun new risen to shed
    Health on human suffering.

Lo! to grant a pardon free,
    Comes a willing Lamb from Heaven;
Sad and tearful, hasten we,
    One and all, to be forgiven.

Once again He comes in light,
    Girding earth with fear and woe;
Lord! be Thou our loving Might,
    From our guilt and ghostly foe.

To the Father, and the Son,
    And the Spirit, who in Heaven
Ever witness, Thee and One,
    Praise on earth be ever given.

                    JOHN HENRY NEWMAN.

The number of Thine own complete,
    Sum up and make an end;
Sift clean the chaff, and house the wheat;
    And then, O Lord, descend.

Descend, and solve by that descent
    This mystery of life;
Where good and ill, together blent,
    Wage an undying strife.

For rivers twain are gushing still,
    And pour a mingled flood;
Good in the very depths of ill,
    Ill in the heart of good.

The last are first, the first are last,
    As angel eyes behold;
These from the sheep-cote sternly cast,
    Those welcomed to the fold.

                    JOHN HENRY NEWMAN.

Great were his fate who on the earth should linger,
    sleep for an age and stir himself again,
watching Thy terrible and fiery finger
    shrivel the falsehood from the souls of men.

Oh, that Thy steps among the stars would quicken!
    oh, that thine ears would hear when we are dumb!
Many the hearts from which the hope shall sicken,
    many shall faint before Thy kingdom come.

Lo! for the dawn (and wherefore wouldst thou screen it?)
    lo! with what eyes how eager and alone,
seers for the sight have spent themselves, nor seen it,
    kings for the knowledge, and they have not known.

                    FREDERIC W. H. MYERS.

6

THIRD WEDNESDAY.

GRIEF.

How shall we sing the Lord's song in a strange land!

IT is easy to sing the Lord's song in the quiet places of home; when life is rising and falling at its ordinary tide; when the sky is familiar above us, and the earth looks as it looked yesterday. When things are *as we are used to.* Not very happy, not very suffering; wearing armor that we have essayed; being *en pays de connaissance.* Then and there, if we are faithful children, we can sing the Lord's song; we can pray, and we can give thanks; and we can feel the actual comfort and presence of the Lord. But in those awful days that come to all—when we find ourselves "in a strange land;" when all the outward and inward land-marks are lost; when we no longer know the sky above us or the earth beneath us for very bewilderment and strangeness; how to sing the Lord's song then?

There are three states into which most of us

(82)

find ourselves sooner or later, and those are : that of sudden and overwhelming grief; that of fiery temptation ; and that of bewildering, unprepared joy.

When sorrow comes, prefaced, perhaps, by a few days of uncertainty and anxiety which we have not recognized as realities, only felt unconsciously, we are bewildered, amazed and wild. The sentence has gone forth, no prayers can stop the fatal process that is begun for our bereavement. All the prayer we can say is, take this cup away. But it cannot be taken away ; it is there for us to drink ; it seems as if a heavy, unfeeling, iron hand were leading us up to where it stood, on an altar shrouded, and dark, and terrible. We must drink, we must submit; we can say what words we choose, they seem to mean absolutely nothing. Not a feeling, not a thought of that dread time, but is new, but is strange, but is to be learned for the first time. We seem to be some one else, praying to some other God. We had thought we had faith.

"Of our heart's preparation we made a romance."

We had thought we knew what we said, when we talked about submission to the will of God. But see ! Does this wild brain, this iron hardness of heart, this mouth dumb of prayer, look like submis-

sion ?   We may never have had doubts before; then
they come in as a flood.   This thing has happened
to us as it happens to all; it might have come sooner
or later, as such or such a circumstance had befallen.
The idea that God's providence has anything to do
with it seems most unreal.   We have been living
in a puerile superstition.   If we had done so or so,
or if that one had been called to help us, it need
not have been.   The heavens above us are brass.
When we most needed God He seems to have failed
us.   Where is God ?   Is there any God ?   What
has all our spiritual life been heretofore ?   Has it
been all an illusion—why are we in this strait ?

Why, God alone knows, who ordered the furnace
to be heated for us.   Such times do not come often
in one life.   Let us brace ourselves to meet the
worst that can possibly befall.   Let us not look for
comfort.   Let us hold fast by God—never let go
our faith, though He slay us.   If words have no
meaning to us any longer, let us still say them.   Let
us say a thousand times a day : "Lord, I submit,
Lord, I submit."   We are consumed by means of
His heavy hand ; but while we have the power of
thought left us, we can bend our souls to acknowl-
edge that it is His hand, and that He has a right

to do what seemeth to Him good. By so much we
have foiled the tempter. If we can have the strength
to sustain ourselves by even this formal profession;
to keep our souls alive through this terrible drought,
by the few drops that we can wring from mental
courage and endurance; if we have not fainted in
this day of adversity; it would seem as if God would
never again doubt us, or put us to this cruel test.
Those who have passed through the fire, may be,
would tell us that there was that burned away that
has made them freer, happier, more heavenly-minded
ever since. That the rest of life has been stamped
with this purification. That the emancipation was
worth the ordeal.

It is wise always to prepare for what must come.
May be if Christians would always, through all their
years of comfort, remember to pray for strength
against the evil day, it would not be so evil; light-
ening down on them out of Heaven in an instant.
There is a prayer of Bishop Wilson which might
daily be added to every one's devotions wisely:
"Remember me, gracious God, in the day of trouble.
Secure me by Thy grace from all excess of fear, con-
cern and sadness." And in this "strange land"
again, let no one look for comfort. Let us try to

endure; try to resist the suggestions of the enemy; keeping fast to simple forms of prayer, remembering that God hears *every word,* though He does not seem to answer; that this can never come to us again. That if we live through this, we shall have a right to be among His own. That it cannot last long; that if we do our part, He will not let us fall, nor let the trial last one instant longer than we can sustain it. There is that about God's laws that would simplify things very much, if we would only set ourselves to study them. We look too far abroad, and miss them. "No *correction* for the time seemeth to be joyous, but grievous. Nevertheless, afterward it yieldeth the peaceable fruit of righteousness." If we could only believe that, and brace ourselves for the grievousness of the time; remembering that if God were over-whelming us with spiritual comforts and graces it would not be correction; and we are being corrected.

"Sufficient for the day is the evil thereof." Again, if we could lay that rule to all our sorrows. Who could not bear a grief one day? Who could not kiss her baby's lips, and lay him in his coffin as calmly as if it were his cradle, if she knew to-morrow she should hold him in her arms again. Well, she may. Mothers have died so soon as that after their little ones were taken from them. Who knows whether God will not have mercy on her to-night? *Only believe.* It is possible to bear a day's separation, a day's loss. Any one who has suffered, will confess it was the looking ahead that was the worst. Is not that really the insupportable thing? God forbids us to look ahead. Take the days as they come; and He will provide the strength to bear all that they may contain.

Again, we cannot believe in God's power to heal. We know that He created our souls as well as our bodies. We have faith to know that that fever-stricken creature, frantic with delirium, will be well, and cool, and sane again, when the disease has run its course; that the ghastly wound on that poor sufferer's body, will slowly, surely, heal itself; that the strange, inexplicable forces of Nature are at work to recreate and reestablish. And yet we cannot trust to God to heal us. Unless we interfere with His work, we shall be healed. "To mortals no sorrow is immortal." *Only believe,* and be patient. Whose are the sweetest, happiest faces? Are they not those that have a widow's cap around them—that have the crape of years about them. Believe, those who have been wounded deepest, have been most fully

healed. Those who have held them fast by God,
have been His peculiar care.

What can we do, o'er whom the unbeholden
　　hangs in a night with which we cannot cope?
what but look sunward, and with faces golden
　　speak to each other softly of a hope?

Can it be true, the grace He is declaring?
　　oh, let us trust Him, for His words are fair!
Man, what is this, and why art thou despairing?
　　God shall forgive thee all but thy despair.

Truly He cannot, after such assurance,
　　truly He cannot and He shall not fail;
nay, they are known, the hours of thy endurance,
　　daily thy tears are added to the tale:

never a sigh of passion or of pity,
　　never a wail for weakness or for wrong,
has not its archive in the angel's city,
　　finds not its echo in the endless song.

Not as one blind and deaf to our beseeching,
　　neither forgetful that we are but dust,
not as from heavens too high for our up-reaching,
　　coldly sublime, intolerably just:—

nay but thou knowest us, Lord Christ, thou knowest,
　　well thou rememberest our feeble frame,
thou canst conceive our highest and our lowest,
　　pulses of nobleness and aches of shame.

Therefore have pity !—not that we accuse thee,
  curse thee and die and charge thee with our woe:
not through thy fault, O Holy One, we lose thee,
  nay, but our own,—yet hast Thou made us so !

Then though our foul and limitless trangression
  grows with our growing, with our breath began,
raise thou the arms of endless intercession,
  JESUS divinest, when thou most art man !

FREDERIC W. H. MYERS.

———

" Sister Sorrow ! sit beside me
Or, if I must wander, guide me ;
Let me take thy hand in mine
Cold alike are mine and thine.

Think not, sorrow, that I hate thee,—
Think not, I am frighten'd at thee,—
Thou art come for some good end,
I will treat thee as a friend.

I will say that thou art bound
My unshielded soul to wound
By some force without thy will
And art tender-minded still.

I will say thou givest scope
To the breath and light of hope,
That thy gentle tears have weight
Hardest hearts to penetrate.

Softly takest thou the crown
From my haughty temples down;
Place it on thine own pale brow
Pleasure wears one,—why not Thou?"

R. M. MILNE.

———

"Sorrow, like the wind
On trees, stirs varying o'er each human mind;
Uprooting some, from some it doth but strew
Blossom and leaf, which spring restores anew;
From some, but shakes rich powers unknown in calm,
And wakes the trouble to extract the balm.
Let weaker natures suffer and despair
Great souls snatch vigor from the stormy air:
Grief, not the languor but the action brings
And clouds the horizon but to nerve the wings."

E. L. BULWER.

THIRD WEDNESDAY.

TEMPTATION.

How shall we sing the Lord's song in a strange land!

WE are always tempted; not an hour passes in which we are free from temptation of some sort—that of the flesh, of the world, of the devil. But we are used to them, and we either yield or resist unconsciously. This is our hourly warfare, our resistance, passing through the enemy's country. But there are times in our life (few, God be praised,) in which we have to know the meaning of the word temptation. It is not walking circumspectly through an enemy's country; it is not watching, resisting, standing firm. It is being subjected, in one short hour, to the assaults of hell; it is finding one's self, by some strange movement of circumstances, in the very heart of the Empire of the Evil One, where we have never been before, where all is strange and fiery, where the ground seems sinking beneath our feet, where all is foreign, bewildering, unsettling. Our whole nature seems changed. We cannot re-

(91)

sist, for our whole nature seems rushing on this fiery
tide of sin. If we abhorred it before, we abhor it
now; but it is master. The means of resistance on
which we have relied before, seem powerless now.
What is the use of moving hand or foot? Nothing
will avail. A sort of dark fatalism possesses us.'
We are dumb. We cannot sing the Lord's song in
this strange land. Our lips refuse to move. One
heart is in a trance. We have never thought of
finding ourselves in this land before. We have not
learned its speech. We do not know whither its
roads lead; what bounds it, what hope there is of
escaping from its limits.

But is this wise, is this right? Are we justified
in such ignorance? Might we not save ourselves by
foresight, by study, from the bewilderment that often leads to defeat. Let us think. It is positive
that to most persons, some one or more crises of
terrible temptation come. Can they be lessened in
power and duration by preparation? It is probable
that they can; the unknown has a vague and mysterious force, and if a thing is looked into it can be
dealt with, ordinarily. Though we cannot know how
we shall be tempted (for our temptation generally
comes when and how we looked not for it) we can

at least teach ourselves what temptation is, and how it is to be combatted. The more fully we recognize our enemy's personal existence, the more sure we are of the ground beneath our feet. That in that spiritual world, which is more real than the world we look upon with our eyes, there is a malicious and fierce master of sin, who is fighting against us personally and in particular, as God, personally and in particular, is defending us and redeeming us. We must not be afraid of him, that is danger ; but we must hate him, must despise him, must cry out against him. It is not enough to pray vaguely against temptation. Cry out for protection against this tyrant. Call him by name in your prayers ; think of how he oppresses you, and spoils your life. Hate him and pray against him, when—

> " With prayer and vow thy soul adorning
> Thou in thy bower salut'st the day."

And at night when the strife is over, and the perils of darkness begin, call God to save you from him and his evil dreams and evil demons. Do not forget him ; that does no good. It is what he works for. Recognize him; keep him clear and distinct before you and resist him. Think how he has got the better of you heretofore, and so be ready with your prayer, your purpose, before he comes again. It is "greatly wise" to think what may be coming and how to meet it.

And it is well to remember, first, how strong he is, and second, how much stronger is He that is with us, and that it is *impossible* for a child of God to fall, unless he consents to fall. It is well to remember, against that time, that God will perhaps not seem to listen to us, that being part of our trial. That every thing will look different to us, and right will seem wrong. But let us hold us fast by God, and know that we are tempted, and that our vision is not clear, and that as right and wrong looked in calm days, so they are in truth. Let us remember how we have been taught, and how we have prayed, and cling to that. Above all, let us pray, though the words seem mockery ; let us pray, and try to trust, though our heart seems empty of faith or love. Make "the sign to angels known ;" bend the knee, say the holy words we have always said. Be not afraid with any amazement. And though, perhaps, you may seem to fall, and your self-esteem is bitterly wounded, when, the assault over, you look back upon it, you will not really have fallen, and your

humiliation will not have been your enemy's
victory.

———

See, when a fire-ship in mid ocean blazes
 lone on the battlements a swimmer stands,
looks for a help, and findeth not, and raises
 high for a moment melancholy hands;

then the sad ship, to her own funeral flaring,
 holds him no longer in her arms, for he
simple and strong and desolate and daring
 leaps to the great embraces of the sea.

So when around me for my soul's affrighting,
 madly red-litten of the woe within,
faces of men and deeds of their delighting
 stare in a lurid cruelty cf sin,

thus as I weary me and long and languish,
 nowise availing from that pain to part,
desperate tides of the whole great world's anguish
 forced through the channels of a single heart;

then let me feel how infinite around me
 floats the eternal peace that is to be,
rush from the demons, for my King has found me,
 leap from the universe and plunge in Thee!
       FREDERIC W. H. MYERS.

THIRD FRIDAY.

JOY.

"How shall we sing the Lord's song in a strange land?"

BUT even as unfamiliar as the land of temptation and the land of woe, is the land of excessive, unanticipated, intoxicating joy. "When hearts are of each other sure." When after disappointment, weariness, pain, there comes "a season of calm weather," a lulling of the winds from every quarter of heaven, bliss and sunshine spreading over all we see, rapture looking down at us out of heaven, care annulled; a covenant made with sorrow; satisfaction; more than content; something beyond happiness. A bewilderment of joy, an overwhelming flood of new life. The temptations to which we have been subject are gone; discontent, despair, faithlessness, we almost forget there ever were such things. What is the use of praying? It is so easy to be good. It is so natural to be thankful. Not in words, nor in express thoughts, but in spirit.

(96)

Our old prayers seem to have lost their meaning; even the words of Holy Scripture seem strange and uncongenial. How can we remember crosses and sufferings, dyings daily, manifold temptations, strength out of weakness, *now?* Even the joy of saints is spiritual joy; and ours, oh! is it all spiritual? Do we long very much for Heaven now? Are we not more than satisfied with earth? That personal, tender love to our only Lord and Saviour JESUS CHRIST? Is it as real, as satisfying as it was? Do we not seem all out of accord with the holy army with whom we have been enrolled? We are almost impatient with the thought that suffering has to be; we want to cancel the rules of our former life; we think it must have been all a great mistake. We want to make a new religion; we write up over our new tabernacle, "Love is the fulfilling of the law." We put far, far out of sight, amid the forgotten archives of our other state, such gloomy words as "through much temptation shall ye enter into the Kingdom of Heaven." "If any man will come after Me let him take up his cross and follow Me." "How hardly shall they that have riches enter into the kingdom of God." "Strait is the gate, and narrow is the way which leadeth

7

unto life, and few there be that find it." All the beatitudes—almost all the Sermon on the Mount, many—oh! how nearly all the words of our Divine Master—must go with them. Ah! whose song are we singing in this strange land? It is so beautiful, this new land, and this new song that fills our hearts, it is so beautiful, and so bewildering too.

Let us remember there are a great many paths that lead away from God; this may be one of them. Let us hold fast our faith, without wavering, and not seek to change it to suit our new condition. Let us not fear happiness, for that is God's gift; but fear ourselves, for we have our part to do. The rule is not altered—life is what it ever was, it is only we who are changed. This great joy will not be forever, there must one day come an end to it; perhaps soon, then we shall have to take up our rejected lessons with heavy hearts and with much loss of progress in them. How shall we make our joy immortal? How sing our tempered, holy song of praise in this tropical and brilliant land? Is it not wise to discipline ourselves, when God is not disciplining us? There is no fear of austerities. Only a little self-denial, a little wearing of the sackcloth of self-renunciation, a little taking up of the cross of sombre thoughts. As many hours a day as ever given to religion, as faithful service as ever in the House of God. No relaxing of the rule, whatever it has been, that has seemed good for our souls before. This will not make the joy less real; it will only hallow it, and make it more reasonable, more safe, less dangerous. If our heart does not seem in the prayers, say them all the same, and add a prayer that the distraction may grow less. Offer thanksgivings, never, never can you offer too many. Put the gratitude into words; do not be contented with the feeling of your heart. Think of all those who are less blessed, and pray for them by name, and earnestly. Be practical, simple, constant in your religion, and you shall still sing the Lord's song, even here. You shall find that earthly joys have not loosened your heart from its immortal allegiance, rather bound it faster. If you have safely withstood the temptations of this state, you are by so much the surer of never falling. You have an experience which has widened your life immeasurably, and which, be it long or short, will never be lost to you, in the existence of your soul.

Hark, how the birds do sing,
    And woods do ring.
All creatures have their joy, and man hath his;
    Yet, if we rightly measure,
    Man's joy and pleasure
Rather hereafter than in present is.

Not that we may not here
    Taste of the cheer;
But as birds drink, and straight lift up their head
    So must he sip and think
    Of better drink
He may attain to after he is dead.

                GEORGE HERBERT.

To be in both worlds full
Is more than God was, who was hungry here.
Wouldst thou His laws of fasting disannul?
    Exact good cheer?
    Lay out thy joy, yet hope to save it?
    Wouldst thou both eat thy cake and have it?

Great joys are all at once;
But little do reserve themselves for more:
Those have their hopes; these what they have renounce,
    And live on score:
Those are at home; these journey still,
And meet the rest on Zion's hill.

Thy Saviour sentenced joy
And in the flesh condemned it as unfit,
At least in lump: for such doth oft destroy;
    Whereas a bit
Doth 'tice us on to hopes of more,
And for the present health restore.

GEORGE HERBERT.

THIRD SATURDAY.

"And thou shalt call his name JESUS."

WHEN this great and saving name was said, for the first time, who, of all the millions of people on the earth, listened to the word? A poor maiden saying her prayers, perhaps in her humble chamber. No one else heard; the angel must have felt the awe and thrill of his great mission as he said the word to her. Priests were standing at the altars of Judea; scribes and lawyers were poring over the books of the Law; great men were bending their minds to this great thought alone, Who was to save this people from their sins, where is the promise of His coming, and when must we look for His appearing. The signs in nature, the portents of the times, were all laid bare, they thought, to the eager eyes of the most learned and most religious of the nation's sons.

But see. One great angel has threaded his way through all the stars they watch so keenly, and they have not seen him. The temple stands on Mount Moriah, but he does not pause; the students by their

(102)

lamps, the great men amid their books,—it is not to them. A poor maiden at her prayers, in all the Jewish world of religion the very humblest member. Oh! if we knew what she had been praying for just then; just then, as the crown of all the ages was held above her brow, and she knew it not! just then, as the eternal thought is imparted to the servant angel; just then, as the word is vibrating through Heaven, that the King has chosen her flesh, her blood, her substance, for His human body. All heaven is flaming with her name, her honor. And she and all earth are silent and unconscious. What thought was she thinking, what prayer was she saying then. O sacred room! O blessed air, in which was first breathed the name of JESUS! Think of that star of light; that first utterance of the name of JESUS, uttered in that lowly room, ascending up on waves of light to heaven; then picture the spreading, widening cloud of glory from that first hour to this; the prayers of saints, the tender calls of loving souls upon His saving name. Think of each call upon Him, as a star fled up to Him; a tiny star gravitating quickly to the nebulæ of its fellows. Millions of the holy race, in martyrdom, in death, in hours of trial, in hours of prayer, in ecstasy, in fear, in love, in yearning tenderness, in gathering gloom, have uttered, upon the unconscious air, millions upon millions of times, the saving name of JESUS. O think of that bright train of light! the mighty radiance of that mass made up of tiny sparks of faith. Think of that path of glory, growing, widening down the steep of heaven, from the first hour to that in which the last saint's cry—

"Come, Lord JESUS!"

shall fill up the measure of the church's part, and He shall come, in answer to their call, along the pathway that their prayers have made.

———

Name of JESUS softly stealing
   O'er a world of strife and shame,
Thou canst bring us heavenly healing,
   O thou all-restoring Name.

They who with the fiend have striven
   Know thy power of comfort well;
JESU'S presence—this is Heaven,
   JESU'S absence—this is Hell.

Name of JESUS! sin assailing
   At thy holy sound shall flee;
Name of JESUS! Sinners wailing
   Find their only rest in thee.

Name of JESUS! oh, how often
Hath the weary child of sin
Felt Thee all his anguish soften,
Shedding Heaven's own peace within.

Those in deadly sickness pining,
Those by pain and fear opprest,
Feel their earthly strength declining,
Yearn to find in Thee their rest.

Name of JESUS, breathing mildly,
Calm the sorrow-burden'd heart,
Still the pulse that beats too wildly,
Bid all restless fears depart.

Name of JESUS! make us holy,
Name of JESUS! make us pure;
Teach us to be meek and lowly,
Teach us humbly to endure.

Name of JESUS! heaven of gladness,
Cause our doubts and fears to cease;
Soothe away this aching sadness,
Name of JESUS! give us peace.

MARY DUNLOP MOULTRIE.

———

Is there not wrong too bitter for atoning?
what are these desperate and hideous years?
hast Thou not heard Thy whole creation groaning—
sighs of the bondsmen, and a woman's tears?

Yes, and to her, the beautiful and lowly,
　　Mary, a maiden, separate from men,
camest thou nigh and didst possess her wholly,
　　close to thy saints, but thou wast closer then.

Once and forever didst thou show thy chosen,
　　once and forever magnify thy choice;—
Scorched in love's fire or with his freezing frozen,
　　lift up your heart, ye humble, and rejoice!

Not to the rich He came and to the ruling,
　　(men full of meat, whom wholly He abhors,)
not to the fools grown insolent in fooling
　　most, when the lost are dying at the doors;

nay, but to her who with a sweet thanksgiving
　　took in tranquillity what God might bring,
blessed Him and waited, and within her living
　　felt the arousal of a Holy Thing.

Ay, for her infinite and endless honor
　　found the Almighty in this flesh a tomb,
pouring with power the Holy Ghost upon her,
　　nothing disdainful of the Virgin's womb.

F. W. H. Myers.

To hang transfixed upon the bitter cross,
To bear Thy bleeding Brows all pierced with thorn,
For frail man's glory to abide foul Scorn,
And for his gain to welcome deepest loss—

This was a Hero's deed.   But to be born
In such poor abject lodging, such scant room,
   A doorless shed in icy blasts forlorn,
So low to stoop, who from such height didst come—
   Oh, what a choice was this, my Sovran Lord?
What strength did Godhead to Thy Cradle lend?
   To bear that outrage of cold winter's breath.
Not more Thy bloody Sweat, or Body gored:
For greater far the distance to descend
   From God to Man, than from poor Man to Death.
      (From the Spanish.)

EDWARD CHURTON.

THIRD SUNDAY.

AMONG the trials of our Lord's life, few seem harder than that conspicuous one, the *enmity*, open and secret, of those among whom He moved; the treachery of some, the contempt of many, the machinations of more, the disfavor of all but a fraction of the Jewish people. The whole of His ministry is marked by this cruel temptation; the last hours of His earthly life were but the consummation of it, the culmination and climax of pursuing hatred. How shall we turn this part of our Lord's sufferings to a lesson for ourselves? Many of us may never have been hated, may never have had to suffer any persecution from without. The times are Christian; the lives of most are shielded and calm; our enemies seem to be they of our own household, they that dwell in our own hearts. But it is hardly possible that we have never had to meet an unkind eye, to be silent under an unjust accusation, to writhe under a treachery of the heart. To be misinterpreted, mis-

(108)

understood, unappreciated, undervalued; to smart under some careless malicious tongue, even though it may be a jesting one. These seem very humble ways of bearing our Lord's sorrows, following afar off indeed. But may be it is all He asks of us in this part of our discipline. If we would arm ourselves for this conflict, or for the direr that may be sent, let us remember these two things, that humility and innocence are our safeguards. If we can get to a state of true humility, of humility that goes through and through our very being, no reproach can add to our self-abasement, no calumny can hurt our pride; to be utterly humble is to be free from the tortures of self-consciousness and its train of manifold miseries. The shafts of most enemies will not hurt us if we have this shield. And if our lives are innocent—innocent of flagrant sins, and searched and guarded by an anxious conscience, surely, no stab in the dark will wound us mortally, no persecution of malice will make us afraid.

———

To be thought ill of, worse than we deserve,
  To have hard speeches said, cold looks displayed,
By those who should have cheer'd us when we swerve,
  Is one of Heaven's best lots, and may be made

A treasure ere we know it, a lone field
Which to hot hearts may bitter blessings yield.
    Either we learn from our past faults to shrink,
When their full guilt is kept before our eye,
    And thinking of ourselves as others think,
We so are gainers in humility:
Or the harsh judgments are a gloomy screen,
    Fencing our altered lives from praise and glare;
And plants that grow in shades retain their green,
    While unmeet sternness kindly cheers the air
F. W. FABER.

Strive to agree.   Life is too full of woe
To cause one needless ache from word unkind,
Or hard cold tone which lingers on the mind:—
Rather a bridge of loving-kindness throw
Over the gap of differing views below.
So may'st thou pass unharming and unharm'd
To safer shores of bright agreement charm'd,
Where the white lily of pure peace doth grow.
For trifles this:—in principle ne'er yield!
Be firm!   Be brave!   Like The One Ark outride
The surging waves of Error's whelming tide.
Let Truth, if need be, with thy blood be seal'd,
Yet pause in every strife, clearly to see,
Right and not victory, thine aim to be!
ANON.

THIRD MONDAY.

The Blind Wayside Beggar.—St. Luke, xix. 35.

In the outskirts of Jericho, a blind man sat by the side of a road begging. Poor wretch; poor as well as blind. How strange and exciting to hear the tumult, the tramp of many feet, to know not at all what the multitude meant, what had brought them together; what way were they going, and who led them on! Perhaps he had a fear of personal danger, and was relieved of a dread, when some kind person answered his question, and said,

"Jesus of Nazareth passeth by."

Oh think of the mighty impulse which must have come upon him, a hope, and such a hope. Maybe he had heard that others had been cured of just such a black sorrow, by this new prophet, whose feet even now stirred the dust of this arid road, where he had sat, so many hateful hours, and begged.—Never before for sight, only for humble alms. Perhaps the prophet would never come this

(111)

way again, this was his one moment of hope, his opportunity. No one else could do for him what he asked, no one in all the world. And *He* never after this moment perhaps. Here was the golden moment of all his life. Think of the sudden strength with which he must have stretched out his arms into the dark vacancy before him and cried,

"JESUS, thou son of David, have mercy on me."

Those that went before tried to hush his cries. Impertinent and hardened time-servers, who thought only, for the moment, of the great man whom they followed, and whom they had not yet turned upon and given up to death. This man must hold his peace, wretched pauper. But he cried so much the more,

"Thou Son of David, have mercy on me!"

Oh! if He should pass by and not heed him, and the hum of the multitude should die away in the distance and there should be no one left beside him, it would be darker for him in his darkness than ever before, stiller in his life-long silence.— Health, sight, healing, were passing before him, passing on, and he could not arrest them, clutching out he only beat the air; no wonder that he cried the more. But JESUS heard him, and standing, ordered that he be brought to Him. And asked him, (blessed question, who would not tremble if he heard it?)

"What wilt thou that I shall do unto thee?"

Ah! how is it with us? We have all our answer ready: it would not be that our sins might be forgiven, that our souls might be saved; it would be the relief from some personal calamity, the bestowal of some earthly gift. The poor beggar asks his sight; that is all the world to him. Blessed, patient Lord, who knoweth whereof we are made, who remembereth that we are but dust! And while He has the Kingdom of Heaven in His gift, only pities us when we ask for Earth, and when He can, gives it to us. Oh! the difference between our prayers, when we ask for heavenly things, and when we ask for earthly. Who ever asked for faith, or hope, or charity, as they have asked for safety in a moment of personal peril, or for the life of a friend, or for the granting of some boon that seemed for the instant of the last importance. And yet, all these things are but for to-day, and all the others (which we might have for the asking; there is no limit *there*); are for the long, long days of heaven. —Let it be our effort to keep before our mind the

8

unseen, and the ever glorious: to moderate our passion for the seen, and the fading. The effort must always ennoble and purify the mind. The reverse always narrows and chills it. One hour each day, spent faithfully in the effort to think of eternity, would without fail show its fruits in a calmer, purer, broader tone of thought. And for the eternal record, perhaps that hour would be the only one in all the twenty-four that would shine upon us with comfort when the books are opened. Our busy duties—oh! how much of them are only miserable egotisms, absolute temptations, things that then we may be glad to have forgotten.

Be of good comfort, rise: He calleth thee!
 When life seems drear and dull,
And loneliness is spread around thy path,
 And thick and plentiful
The thorns of sorrow lie: be sure He hath
Some special work for Him whereto He calleth thee.

Be of good comfort, rise: He calleth thee!
 O vexed, O weary soul,
Call thou on JESUS as He passeth by,
 And He will make thee whole:
For He hath borne the Cross of Calvary,
That thou may'st bear the Cross whereto He calleth thee.

Be of good comfort, rise: He calleth thee!
  Though blind thine eyes may be
As thou sitt'st pleading by the way alone,
    Yet cry—"Look Thou on me,
Have mercy on me, JESU, David's Son!"
Then shalt thou hear that voice: "Arise! He calleth thee."

Be of good comfort, rise: He calleth thee!
  Cease not thy fainting breath,
Though many neighbors bid thee hold thy peace,
    For He of Nazareth
Unto the heavy-laden brings release;
E'en now He passeth by: Arise! He calleth thee.

Be of good comfort, rise: He calleth thee!
  Thy life, may be, is still;
Thy duty in the homely vulgar round;
    Perhaps it is His will,
That there thy service may by Him be crowned,
And thou may'st learn that, though unseen, He calleth thee.

Be of good comfort, rise: He calleth thee!
  When men deride thy part,
And faithful love is mock'd by worldly spite,
    Remember, weary heart,
That thou art not the first to bleed from it:
He bled, for thirty years unknown, Who calleth thee.

Be of good comfort, rise: He calleth thee!
  Cast all thy bonds away
The world's loose garments round both breast and limb,
    Lest aught may thee delay

When thou art hastening blind and halt to Him:
Arise, O weary soul; arise! He calleth thee.

GERARD MOULTRIE.

My sins are deep and many as the seas;
Yet hear, as Thou art wont, Thy suppliant's call;
And by the Power of Thy Most Holy Keys
    Loose me from all!

With trembling heart I venture to Thy Gate
For sins committed and for broken laws,
O LAMB OF GOD, the Sinner's Advocate,
    Plead Thou my cause!

Set not my sins before Thy Face, nor lay
My vileness to my charge, for I am Thine:
O LAMB OF GOD, that takest sin away,
    Take away mine!

The Holy Creed delivered to the Saints
I steadfastly believe: my faith increase;
Make strong my Love, confirm my hope that faints,
    And give me peace!

So grant me absolution in my need,
That I, who only to Thy mercy flee,
May henceforth live with wariness and heed,
    Or die to Thee.

Glory to Thee, Who didst at first create,
Glory to Thee, Whose passion maketh whole,
Glory to Thee, Who didst regenerate
    Thy servant's soul!

J. M. NEALE.

THIRD TUESDAY.

THE GOOD SHEPHERD.

How many times our Lord refers to the vocation and duties of a shepherd—how constantly He calls us His Flock. That pastoral, thoughtful, unworldly sort of life makes the simile more acceptable to us than any other would have been. In storms and tempests, on dark nights and in stern dangers, the shepherd is alone with his flock; they have none else to look to, and he has no companion but these inferior ones. He loves them, for whatever reason, and lays down his life for them.

How shall we make our Shepherd love us? Not with the general, protecting care that He has for all His flock, but with the individual tenderness that He has for one that He has borne in His bosom and nurtured with His arm. There is a way: by abasing ourselves at His feet—by casting ourselves upon His love, following closely after Him—by loving Him personally, tenderly, actually.

(117)

No doubt He likes our service, but He likes our love better, our worship, our secret thoughts, our inner duty, of which we do not think that it is duty. O God of might! Give us this heart—give us the lamb-like humble nature that will make us lovely to our Lord. Let Him see of the travail of His soul and be satisfied. Let love fill our hearts; let humility be the mark of our lives.

———

Weep not for them who weep
    For friend or lover taken hence, for child,
That falls 'mid early flowers and grass asleep,
    Untempted, undefiled.

Mourn not for them that mourn
    For sin's keen arrow with its rankling smart,
God's hand will bind again what He hath torn,
    He heals the broken heart.

But weep for him whose eye
    Sees in the midnight skies a starry dome
Thick sown with worlds that whirl and hurry by,
    And give the heart no home;

Who hears amid the dense
    Loud trampling crash and outcry of this wild,
Thick jungle world of drear magnificence,
    No voice which says, *my child.*

Who marks through earth and space
A strange dumb pageant pass before a vacant shrine.
And feels within his inmost soul a place
Unfilled by the Divine;

Weep, weep, for him above
That looks for God, and sees unpitying Fate,
That finds within his heart, in place of love,
A dull, unsleeping hate.

DORA GREENWELL.

FOURTH WEDNESDAY.

St. John, ii. 1.

In a life of thirty-three years, is not this the only record of our Master's presence at a feast; except the feast in the house of Simon, where Mary anointed His feet, "against the day of His burial," and the feast in the upper chamber, which He turned into a banquet for all the generations of the Children of Men, till that great gala-day of Heaven and Earth when He shall come again. The first feast, He glorifies and makes bountiful, He works a generous miracle that cheers and makes glad the heart of man; in this bright and beneficent way He manifests Himself to His disciples, and binds them to Him believingly. How little of self there is in this; though He is the great self; the centre of all the universe.

To take our humble lesson from Him; might we not go into the bright places of the world, if

(120)

we went with the mind with which He went? Might we not mix with the world, if we only thought of it without reference to ourselves? If we could carry with us only a remembrance of our own personality, strong enough to make us believe that we could help some one that might be less fortunate, and less prepared; brighten and cheer the scene by some gift we may possess; see in pleasure only cause for thankfulness. Oh! if our hearts were pure, how lovely the world would be! How sweet the pleasures of life! Good Lord! Is it in vain to hope we may ever reach the point of purity, where gay scenes will bring no snare—where mirth will never weaken faith—where the sight of others' joy will ever give delight?

And one needs to be a saint to go into scenes, the air of which is filled with subtle poison that enters by every diseased and uncauterized spot in our souls. Envy, detraction, vanity, levity, verily one seldom brings home a white conscience from the house of rejoicing. And yet surely this need not be. But oh! the axe must be laid at the root of the tree. The thought and intention of self-sacrifice must be the first thought and intention of our souls. It is the only safety; for where

there is self, there is sin. While we think of ourselves, and desire to see ourselves advanced, the
sight of others' beauty, wealth, success, will turn
into the sin of envy while we look. Our tongues
will carry out the rancor in our hearts; we shall
have spread abroad the poison we have bred. If we
are thinking of ourselves, and longing for praise,
and coveting admiration, the least word or look will
light the miserable, garish lights of vanity, and
make an end of all the delicate hues and tints of
modesty. Think of all the sins of feasts, little
and great. Each grand entertainment, what a
heap of sins to be laid before its door as the
débris. Generally a wrong or selfish intention at
the start; at best, a compliance with a worldly
code of obligations. Then, not even is the pleasure of others our effort, only as it reflects upon
ourselves. Do we ask those whom no one else
asks? Do we ask those whom truly we respect,
and who make us better? Do we think about any
law but the law of society, when we select our
guests, and make ready for the exercise of that
sacred work of hospitality of which the Bible says
so much? Then, the petty cares, the fret of *con-
tretemps*, the distraction of mind. How many

prayers blurred, how many meditations done away
with; how many little duties and graciousnesses
omitted; how many sharp and impatient words
spoken! Enough care and earnestness to prepare
a good death-bed; as much thought and infinitely
more circumspection than ever goes to a preparation for an Easter, a Christmas Communion.
Then the money spent in so many hurried, reckless ways—how would it compare with the open-
handedness of our charities? What would it do
towards paying for the education of some boy,
whose mother's heart is sore with the tight bands
of poverty; towards making sure a shelter for
some brood of little children, whose sick and worn-
out father spends days in working feebly for, and
nights in planning hopelessly about?

Not for thyself thy motherhood,
   Nor for thy home that life-stream springs;
For thee, then, too, the higher good
   Must come through death of lower things.

The village home so sweet to thee,
   With joys so hallow'd and complete,
For Him no Father's House could be,
   No limit for thy Saviour's feet.

The will long meekly bow'd to thine
 Now calmly claims its sovereign place,
And takes a range of love Divine
 Thy mortal vision cannot trace.

On us that mild reproof falls cold,
 The words, and not the tone, we hear;
On thee, who knewest Him of old,
 It casts no shade of doubt or fear.

For thy meek heart has read Him true,
 And, bowing, wins His "rather bless'd."
"Whate'er He saith unto you, do,"
 Embracing as its rule and rest.

Then through earth's ruins heav'n shines bright;
 The widest sphere, the dearest home,
Save that where Christ is Lord and Light,
 Were but at last the spirit's tomb.

Thus, laying down thy special bliss,
 Thou winnest joy, all joy above,
The endless joy of being His,
 And sharing in His works of love.

       MRS. CHARLES.

———

The Hand that strews the earth with flowers
 Enrich'd the marriage feast with wine;
The Hand once pierced for sin of ours
 This morning made the dew-drops shine;

Makes rain-clouds palaces of art,
  Makes ice-drops beauteous as they freeze;
The heart that bled to save—that heart
  Sends countless gifts each day to please;

Spares no minute refining touch
  To paint the flower, to crown the feast,
Deeming no sacrifice too much;
  His care and leisure for the least;

Gives freely of its very best,
  Not barely what the need may be,
But for the joy of making bless'd—
  Teach us to love and give like Thee!

Not narrowly men's claims to measure,
  But question daily all our powers;
To whose cup we add a pleasure?
  Whose path can we make bright with flowers?

MRS. CHARLES.

FOURTH THURSDAY.

---◆---

THANKFULNESS.

OUR nature makes this virtue harder than it at first looks. First, for the reason that in prosperous times, when there seems most cause for gratitude, all experience goes to prove our hearts are duller and harder than in days of trouble. And in days of trouble there seems so little cause for gratitude, and our dead baby or our lost fortune or our fractured limb, blot out the memory of our long exemption from these troubles, and our many mercies left, our long eternity of bliss to come, the great work of salvation, and the marvels that surround us. Perhaps the malicious enemy tries to quench the flame of the little lamp of praise that should be always burning, night and day, in storm and shine, before the altar of sacrifice in our hearts.—Sure it is,—it often goes out in those Christian shrines. O when our Lord looks down, how many, do you suppose, does He find burning! What sorrow to Him, to see that His Priesthood of suffering and temptation—His stained Cross—His open grave, cannot compensate us for some short-lived pain ; cannot rouse us to more than a few hours of thanksgiving. What more can He do for us than He has done ?

What more can we do for Him than we have done ? We can praise him. On our knees. In the congregation. By our words. By our thoughts. Formally, and in unconscious acts, outwardly, and in our unuttered thoughts. We can study to be grateful. We can recall His mercies to us as His children, and to us as His people. We can count over our personal blessings, and our part in the Great Redemption. All this is to be done as an effort of the will, as a matter of devotion, not to be left to the chance emotions of the hour. It is our part to correct and overcome temperament, and the fate of circumstances. We cannot be too grateful, so we may use all spiritual arts to foster this great virtue without danger of falling into sin.

Prayer benefits ourselves,—praise benefits God. He asks for it ; His word is full of exhortations to it. He chooses it ; it is the simple payment He asks. O why cannot we run to Him with it, why cannot we fill His ear with our praises, till His soul blesses us—Oh ! why are we contented with being just saved. Why are we satisfied to be far-off servants, when we might be darlings of our Lord's inmost heart—S. Johns. S. Marys. Glorious and beautiful saints of God, instead of hardly-saved, duty-doing children of the law. God fill us with thanksgiving, cover us with the garment of praise in the days of darkness as well as in the hours of joy!

———

Go, tell the roaring sea,
    And tell the desert sands,
And bid the wild winds see
    Thine anguish-wringing hands;
And bid the forked lightnings brood
Black over men's ingratitude.

Tell of the sick, the nursed
    Who left thee in thy need;
Tell of the mob accursed,
    Who mock'd thy patriot deed;
Tell of the king who owed his breath
To thee, and lets thee starve to death.

Tell of thy children's hate,
    Thy friend's averted eye,
Thy brother's traitorous fate,
    Thy wife's adultery;
And echo sad will sigh abroad,
What hast thou been thyself to God?

FROM "POEMS OF BY-GONE YEARS."

My heart is fix'd on One above,—
To win His smile, to please His eyes
My heart is fain : because I love,
I serve,—nor yet with tears and sighs ;
By patient duty love must rise,—
And late and early, far and near
I sought Him gifts ; to him are dear
The things that others still despise.

I sought for Him in Spring-time cold,
The trembling palm that comes in haste,
The little crocus all in gold,
The slender snow-drop, and the bold,
Mezereon, on its leafless stem :
Fair things that do not fear to waste
Their gentle souls ! and after them
Another store I chanced to find
Of things forgotten, left behind.

Some soft white fleece by briers torn
From off the flock,—some ear of corn,
Dropt careless from the gleaner's breast,
The last red berry on the thorn,
Or prize of some forsaken nest.

There came on earth a weary time ;
If this be Autumn, where is now
The fruit upon the laden bough,
The harvest redd'ning in the broad
Calm sunshine, where the squirrels' hoard,

9

The winding clear of hunter's horn ?
Leaves only, wither'd leaves I found ;
A mournful silence, mornful sound
Of wind that rustled through the sere,
Stark boughs, and from the shrunken ear
Shook out the thin and blighted corn.

But while I mourn'd thereat, more clear
Than song of bird at Autumn eve,
A voice was borne upon mine ear,
A voice that said, " Why wilt thou grieve,
And must I still from thee receive ?
How hast thou learnt which pleaseth best—
The gift thou bringest, or the free,
Firm open palm held up to me ?
The less is of the greater blest.

" *Remember what on earth I spake.*"
" Oh ! then," I said, " at this Thy word
I take Thee now, through zeal I erred,
Through love, that bids me now confess
My fault ; to give be Thine ! to bless
Is Thine ; dear Lord, to Thee I leave
The greater blessing ! with the less,
So well content I will not grieve
From Thee for ever to receive.

" And still receive ! and never cease
To gaze on all this wealth of Thine,
To joy in all Thy flocks' increase,

Far more than if my cup with wine
And oil ran o'er, and store of wheat
In finest flour, and honey sweet
From out the stony rock were mine!"

" To give than to receive more blest!"
Thou saidest. "Oh! Thou Giver free!
Good measure, shaken down and press'd
Together, now I ask from Thee;
Oh! give to me, dear Lord, and still
Increase Thy boons! make broad the place
Where Thou dost dwell in me, and fill
My hands with gifts, my heart with grace;
But let me look upon Thy face.
What need to mourn if Thou on mine
But little comeliness should trace
When love can give me all of Thine?
The loved are fair, the loved are dress'd
In garments rich and fresh and rare.
  Oh! bless Thou me and I am blest.
  Oh! love Thou me and I am fair!"

DORA GREENWELL.

———◆———

St. Matt. xix, 16, S. Mark. x, 17, S. Luke, xviii, 18,

Our Lord had just been blessing little children, and had been holding them in His arms, with words of love. A young man, of noble and pure heart, living honorably in the midst of wealth and power, seeing this beautiful sight, is filled with admiration, and comes running to Him, and kneeling down, asks Him:

"Good Master, what shall I do that I may inherit eternal life?" As if he had said, "You have promised it to these children, who have done nothing. Behold me, who have done what I could according to my lights. What more shall I do, to be served as they?"

Verily, do as they do, love not the world nor the things that are in the world. Have a pure, simple, detached heart. Have faith. Put yourself on a level with them, make yourself nothing—a child —a beggar—at God's feet. Then Jesus tests his

(132)

faith; "Why callest thou Me good. There is none good but God."

He does not reply; he is not sure that this gracious prophet is more than a prophet. Then our Lord rehearses to him the commandments as regarding our duty to our neighbor. The young ruler says, with truth and a clear conscience:

"All these have I kept from my youth up. What lack I yet?" Ah! then the knife struck to the heart of the disease, the ulcer on this fair, pure flesh.

"*If thou wilt be perfect*, go and sell that thou hast, and give to the poor, and thou shalt have treasure in heaven; and come and follow me."

Perhaps he did not will to be perfect, only very good and very honorable, and very strictly a righteous man towards men. Perhaps the surroundings of his life had encrusted themselves about him, till he could not separate himself from them, he could not think of himself as other than the rich young ruler, who was using his rank and his wealth so well. He could not lay down these weapons, this great influence, these gifts; what good could he do, as a nameless beggar, following this homeless prophet through the villages and towns of Judea? His

family, his name, he owed them something. He
was too much entangled with the things of this life.
Ah! poor young warrior. We cannot tell what had
the greatest influence upon him, among these con-
siderations; all we know is, he was not ripe for
JESUS' call, as the fishermen on the shore of Galilee
were. He had more chains about him: links of gold
and silver (the links we pray for, and long for, and
thank God for when they come). He had come running to Christ, full of admiration and zeal. He goes
slowly away, very sorrowful. For he had great pos-
sessions. But JESUS had loved him when He looked
on him; and let us believe that that love drew him
back to him, even as the look of JESUS cast on S.
Peter, drew him back to truth.

For ourselves, let this be the lesson. Never to
neglect any call of Christ's, even though it be one
that demolishes our whole structure and purpose of
life. Never to forget the different value of the two
kinds of coin that are passing through our hands;
the pure metal that will stand the fire of the day of
doom; and the baser metal that is to perish with the
using. Let every day have a few moments of
thought contrasting time and eternity.

THE SAYING OF ST. HERMAS.

"Concupisce opus tuum, et salvus eris."

The whole world hath gone out to buy,
Estates and goods to multiply:
The sunny field, the garden ground,
The woods that gird the city round,
The cedar hall, the ample street,
The quay where busy merchants meet,
All places and all spirits burn,
And for the world's weak treasure yearn,

Servant of Christ! be thou like these,
All day and night forego thine ease;
Crave, covet, lust, and labor still,
Till thou the Master's storehouse fill.
Be crafty at thy toil, and ply
All seasons round the usury.
Deny thyself, and hoard thy gold
For Him who died for thee of old.

Let not thy life be soft and free,
Cushion and couch are not for thee.
Brave shining stone and raiment fair
Leave thou for kings and priests to wear.
For them let rich robes be unfurled
Who bear God's name within the world,
Thy throne, O man of God, is yet
Behind thick clouds and trials set.

Let go all mortal grief and mirth;
And, as the world is wise for earth,
To thee like wisdom shall be given
To covet still and hoard for heaven.
Empty on priests, and heathen lands,
And widows pale, thy willing hands;
While prince and peer of old names dream,
Let alms thy sin-pledged soul redeem.

Wide, Christian! is thy mother's field,
A hundred-fold her valleys yield,
Hoard, and then waste; oh! scatter round
Thy seed in faith upon the ground,
When men are deep in feast and mirth,
Steal out and bury gold in earth,
Then back into the world and ply
Once more thy hard trade cheerily.

                               F. W. FABER.

FOURTH SATURDAY.

THE Jews sent the priests to St. John the Baptist to ask him, who he was. The prophet gave no uncertain answer: he was not the Christ, he was not Elias. He was only the humble runner before the chariot of the great King—only the voice to give warning of His coming: nothing, absolutely nothing in himself, noted as had been his birth, and holy as had been his life, great as were his gifts. This was in Bethabara beyond Jordan where he was baptizing. The day after the visit of the priests from Jerusalem at which St. John had made his confession of inferiority, and had announced that He whom' they sought was standing among them, he saw our Lord approaching him and exclaimed, "Behold the Lamb of God which taketh away the sin of the world!"

Perhaps his eyes were just then opened, after his humble and devout confession, for a little farther on he says, "And I knew Him not." Oh! to have been on the banks of the Jordan that day! To

(137)

have heard the great Prophet proclaim the words then for the first time uttered on Earth, foreshadowing the Sacrifice, the Redemption. S. Mary had kept all the words in her heart that had been uttered by the angel, by the aged Simeon and Anna, by the gracious Child Himself, but we are not told that any of those words were indicative of the manner in which He was to accomplish the Salvation of His people.—Perhaps till the Baptist looked on Him that day, the thought had never been thought on Earth, except in the Divine Mind, that it was by Death that the salvation was to come.

"He shall drink of the brook in the way, therefore shall He lift up His head." The time had come for Him to begin His life's work: this was His birth into the spiritual Kingdom which He had prepared for us from the foundation of the world— "His better birthday." Our Bodies,—by His Birth, —our Souls by His Baptism,—our Spirits—by His Death,—purchased and redeemed and made His forever. How blessed the Baptist, who was permitted to receive our Lord into the Church. How like to the honor of the Virgin, who was permitted to bear Him in the flesh. And how strange, that of these two, He should have spoken those cold and repressing words, "He that is least in the Kingdom of God is greater than he." And, " Yea, rather blessed are they that hear the word of God and keep it." "For whosoever shall do the will of my Father which is in Heaven, the same is my brother, and sister, and mother."

What lesson should we learn from that?—That the place in Heaven has nothing to do with the place on earth; except so far as it has been used as a means for spiritual advancement. That God's gifts are not so precious as His graces, and that His graces are won by our own will, joined to and working with His holiest will.

Work out your own salvation, though it is God that worketh in you to will and to do of His good pleasure. He has put it into our own hands; may He give us grace to profit by His gifts.

————

Hail, O thou of women born
 Highest station claiming,
By the Holy Angel called
 "John" on day of naming;
Hallow'd from thy mother's womb,
 Herald-beacon lighted
To give light to them that sit
 In death's shades benighted.

Hail, who in the wilderness
    From the world retreating
Didst the camel's hair put on,
    Desert honey eating;
Free from carnal taint of sin,
    Water was thy potion,
Thus the world thou puttest off,
    Putting on devotion.

Hail, thou shepherd sent before
    To prepare the pasture,
With thy finger thou didst point
    To the Lamb thy Master:
At the Jordan thou didst cry
    With the voice of warning,
Telling that the night is past
    Ere Heaven's nearer morning.

Hail, alone of human kind
    To whose charge 'twas given
To baptize the holy head
    Of the Lord of Heaven:
Who didst hear the Father's voice
    That blest rite attending,
Who didst see the Holy Ghost
    As a dove descending.

Hail, bright rosebud blushing red
    With thy Passion's flower,
Lily sweet of chastity
    For life's sunset hour;

May thy voice yet cry aloud
    With its warning sentence,
When Heaven's kingdom is at hand
    Calling to repentance.

                    GERARD MOULTRIE.

_____

Also of John a calling and a crying
    rang in Bethabara till strength was spent,
cared not for counsel, stayed not for replying,
    John had one message for the world, Repent.

John, than which man a grander or a greater,
    not till this day has been of woman born,
John, like some iron peak by the Creator
    fired with the red glow of the rushing morn.

This when the sun shall rise and overcome it
    stands in his shining desolate and bare,
yet not the less the inexorable summit
    flamed him his signal to the happier air.

                    FREDERIC W. H. MYERS.

FOURTH SUNDAY.

HUMILITY.

HUMILITY is a thorough abasement of one's self, before God, before man, in one's own soul. It is a grace without which it is impossible to be a Christian. It is a condition of mind about which there is a great deal of self-deception; the hardest thing in the world is to be humble; and the easiest thing in the world is to think that one is humble. No Christian can begin to search his own heart I believe, without being amazed at the unsuspected growth of pride which covers everything he finds there. The insidious weed is clinging to his motives; why does he do this magnanimous, kind act to one who has injured him? Because it is nobler and higher toned to do it; because his self-respect requires it; because as one who desires to lead an honorable life and respect himself as well as be respected, it must be done, and he knows he shall be happier. It is not a passionate prostration at the foot of the Cross : "Lord, I have sinned a thousand-fold more deeply than this enemy of mine. A hundred years of penance could not wash out my sins; I am not worthy to ask this favor at thy hands; but forgive me for Christ's sake, and forgive him."

It has crept over and almost hidden from his sight his worse and baser actions. Was that a sin? O but it was the sin of a grand impulsive, passionate nature: Lord I thank thee that I am not as other men are, even in my sins. Was *that* a selfish action? The instinct of nature; and I cannot help it if I see so clearly and so quickly; duller people have not the same temptation. Do I shrink from others and hold myself from them? It is because I am not "altogether of such clay;" they may be a great deal better than I am, but we are not alike (and in my heart I am thankful we are not). And so on through an endless, endless search. Pride has grown thickly over all; pride has given the tone, the color to all, till we do not recognize the difference between good and bad. Only by constant searching, by bringing our motives to the light, and tearing away the deceit that has so long fattened on them, can we convict ourselves, and gain that fragrance of humility that is as incense in the eyes of our Great God, "once made for us so low."

Is it not amazing that children of that King, crowned with thorns and wearing a purple robe, should dare hold in their inmost hearts a thought of *pride*. Would it not seem as if that Crown, that Robe, would have killed forever the ugly shape of Pride ; that once for all it had trailed along the way of Sorrow, and had pressed the brow of a King; and that in Christendom for evermore it would be dead ? Alas! To attain humility, it would seem as if but two things were necessary ; to look at Christ's life on earth ; and to look into our own hearts. To look at our neighbors' lives is not what will help us ; but *to pray*, will.

———

"The meek shall increase their joy in the Lord."

———

So spake the hoary thyme,
　　Half hidden in the grass;
I watch from morning prime
　　Until my Lord shall pass.

How bright beneath the sun,
　　How sweet within the glade,
The flow'rets ope, each one
　　Beloved by Him who made
His flowers that live in light
　　His flowers that live in shade.

The primroses are pale,
  Yet fair; the violet grows
Beneath her leafy veil,
  And be she pale none knows,
Or be she fair, so sweet her soul
  that overflows.

But all my head is strew'd
  With ashes gray; and bent
Beneath the footfall rude,
  Steals forth my timid scent,
Crushed from a leaf that curls its wound
  to hide content.

Why should my Lord delight
  In me? Behold how fair
His garden is! How bright
  His roses blow'ng there;
His lilies all like queens, that know not
  toil nor care.

In white calm peace on high
  Each rears a blossom'd rod;
The gentian low doth lie,
  Yet lifts from up the sod
An eye of steadfast blue, that looks up
  straight to God.

I wait my Lord to greet,
  I can but love and sigh;
I watch His eye to meet,
10

He can but pass me by;
And if His hasty feet
Should crush me, it were sweet
Beneath His feet to die.

DORA GREENWELL.

THE ROTHAY.

(An Extract.)

Thou canst not know, dear Stream! the joy,
Without misgiving or alloy,
Which abstinence and self-control
Spread like a sunrise o'er the soul.
Thou canst not know what flight is given,
Unto the very doors of Heaven,
To hearts which from self-sacrifice,
Like birds from lowly places rise,
Who soar the highest when their mirth
Is humblest on the lowly earth.
Thy song cheers not thyself, dear River!
Because it is a song forever;
It is thyself, thy life, and not
A gift, a separable lot,
Of whose deep tenderness and beauty
Thou canst by self-restraint and duty
Win sweet returns or augmentations;
It hath no daily new creations,
Fresh births which come from sapient glee,
From wisdom, from simplicity,
When mortal joys themselves refrain
For virtue's sake, then flow again.

So are we made; unquiet pleasure,
Which the calm spirit cannot measure,
Endureth not, and is no treasure.
The mirth we cannot put away
Is but a mirth on its first day.
The joy which we cannot restrain
Is but a liberty from pain.
Where self and pleasure are but one,
That soul is morally undone.

F. W. FABER.

FOURTH MONDAY.

On one of His walks of mercy or of meditation, with His disciples following, the Saviour passes a man born blind, and the disciples ask; whose sin caused this? Christ answered, it was not a punishment, but a means of glorifying God. How comforting sometimes to think that our sorrows are not sent as punishments, but as means to glorify God in our bodies and in our spirits, which are His.

And Christ this time did not wait for a supplication from the sufferer. He healed him. A poor wretch that begged, that had never seen the light, nor the face of man. Think how ignorant he must have been, how low in intellect, and how unlovely. And yet he could be the monument of God's power and glory, and could stand before the ages as His witness. Christ anointed his eyes, and then sent him to the pool of Siloam to wash. He went and washed and received his sight. There is the thought of Baptism always brought up by this story. The water that filled this pool,

(148)

flowed from a living spring that is beneath the
Temple vaults, the source of Milton's

"Brook that flowed
Hard by the oracle of God."

Those waters still flow on, making glad the City
of God, the desolated strange sad City of God;
for Mussulman and Jew and Christian alike, if
they will stoop to drink. The waters of Baptism
still flow on; who is the Judge? Whether they
will hear or whether they will forbear; there flows
the healing stream through all the ages.

Then began the disputes and cavils of those
wretched Pharisees. Here was something to resent
indeed; a cure, the like of which has never been
known. Since the man would not deny his bene-
factor, he must be cast out of the congregation of
the righteous. So much can prejudice do in the
service of Satan, wearing God's livery. The pa-
rents of this poor man even doubted, and dared
not sustain him; they perhaps would rather he
had groped on in blindness all his life than have
endangered them with their small coterie, and
caused them to be disgraced in the eyes of men.

How many wise and true things this poor man

said! "God heareth not sinners." "If any man
be a *worshipper* of God and doeth His will, him
He heareth." "If this man were not of God, He
could do nothing." In disgust and indignation
they reproach him with his birth and cast him
out. JESUS *heard that they had cast him out* and
when He had found him, He asked if he believed
on the Son of God.

"Who is He, Lord, that I might believe on
Him?" "Lord, I believe," and he worshipped
Him. This man did not seek JESUS, but twice
JESUS came to him. From this we may learn
two things; first, to pray to God ever to seek us,
never to give us up. Second, to follow His example in seeking those that are out of the way,
and in never ceasing to pray for their salvation,
and to bring them to worship God and be healed.
None are too low, or too lost. How do we know
that God will not save them? And save them
through us.

"No wonder," says a recent writer, "no wonder
that the heart of man should feel strangely yet
sweetly at home in the region of spiritual inter-
vention; no wonder that expiation and the giving up of life for life, that intercession for others

which is but the practical extension of the Atonement, the pouring out of one human soul for another in prayer, even as Christ's soul was poured forth for the world in agony and death, should become the natural language of every heart whose highest energies Divine grace has touched and kindled into life. Intercession is the mothertongue of the whole family of Christ. Here, under whatever other differences,

'Their speech is one
Their witnesses agree.'

" The Saint, be he Catholic or Protestant, bears the world upon his heart, the careless, wicked, suffering world, as Christ bore it upon the cross. He knows that it is still in bondage with its children, but he will agonize for it in the strength of the Saviour whom it has rejected; he knows that it cannot weep over an alienation which it does not feel, but his tears shall flow for it in secret places. The Saint loves the world as Christ loved it, and desires to suffer for it, through an instinct, which tells him that so only can its highest deliverance be wrought out."

There is not on the earth a soul so base
But may obtain a place
In covenanted grace;
So that his feeble prayer of faith obtains
Some loosening of his chains,
And earnests of the great release which rise
From gift to gift, and reach at length the eternal prize.

All may save self;—but minds that heavenward tower
Aim at a wider power,
Gifts on the world to shower.
And this is not at once; by fastings gain'd
And trials well sustain'd,
By pureness, righteous deeds, and toils of love,
Abidance in the Truth, and Zeal for God above.

J. H. NEWMAN.

THE CROSS.

"A thing of double purpose is the Cross;
A two-edged sword—it hews down or it saves;
A spar—it rescues when wild tempests toss
A rock—it wrecks and sinks beneath the waves.

It is of life a savour unto life;
It is of death a savour unto death;
It leads the van in fierce and bloody strife;
It calms the soul ruffled by passion's breath.

What has no root is burned up by its rays;
What has deep root is sheltered by its shade:
Where faith is not, it blinds by its bright blaze;
When faith is strong, by it the soul is stayed.

It tortured One with direst throes of pain;
  Itself with the life-blood of One it laved;
That all repose in Paradise might gain;
  That all from death and torment might be saved.

To Thee, O most amazing Cross, we cling;
  Thy shame and Thy nails sharp we ask to feel;
Thou dost solution of all mysteries bring;
  Thou art the knife that probes, that it may heal."

A. M.

FOURTH TUESDAY.

Lord, if Thou hadst been here!

SAD trouble had come into the home at Bethany where Christ had found perhaps His only earthly rest. He had no home of His own: He had borrowed this, and so sanctified that yearning of the human heart. The brother is dead. We know very little of Lazarus, except of his earthly fate, that he died ; of his spiritual estate, that JESUS loved him. And of all the three, it is said, that JESUS loved them. St. John records it, who felt the worth of love. Martha attracts us so little: though no doubt she had more respect and consideration from her associates, and though JESUS loved her.

But the divine fragrance of Mary's memory! The holy radiance that surrounds her name! One act of hers, an act of worship, lives enshrined in the Church's oracles to all time. Martha's work, daily, unceasing, self-denying, practical, raises never a thought of emulation or of reverence. Why is this?

(154)

Yet JESUS loved her, though He did not praise her. Her faith was clear and she expressed it well: we hear but few words of Mary's faith. When the dreadful blow fell on them, Martha, restless, goes out to meet the Master of whose coming she hears; and accosts Him with the very words that Mary afterwards uses:

"Lord, if Thou hadst been here my brother had not died."

But Mary sat still in the house. When called to meet Christ, she goes out and meeting Him, falls at His feet. "Lord, if Thou hadst been here!" She worships, with her soul and body. And the sight of her moves Her Master more than the sight of her sister had done. He wept. The thought of all the partings, of all the agonies and desolations, of the last enemy to be conquered, till He should come again in triumph, and bring the lost ones with Him, filled His soul with anguish. He wept for us who are to suffer, who have suffered, who are suffering, and not for her, whose sorrow He was so soon to turn into joy. O tender Saviour! Bless us with those tears and heal our sorrows! They have been shed upon the earth: Thou hast no more tears now, in Heaven; but those, exhaled and falling in dew upon the hearts of those that mourn like Mary, can rise and fall again, and never lose their divine balm and moisture, "till from the East, the Eternal Morning moves." O human-hearted God! Thou knowest the darkness of smitten homes; Thou knowest the appalling weight of gloom that comes with mortal partings: never cease to pour Thy grace and pity in those places where the inevitable blow has fallen! O that our prayers might gain for ourselves, for those we love, for some poor sufferer unknown and only loved through Christ, grace and comfort for the hour of doomed happiness that is slowly perhaps, but surely, coming to the door! Oh! on our knees we pray—for ourselves and for them; what grace we would ask for ourselves we ask for them, comfort, ease, support, high faith in that dread time. Let us feel Thy pity. Let us have unearthly power to look ahead : let us see far into the land of faith. Make our sufferings acceptable to Thee, and let neither soul, nor body, nor brain fail. Let it all be an act of worship, a dread law of Nature turned into a homage, and an honor, to Him who has died, and is alive for evermore.

"There are twelve hours in the day. If any man walk in the day time

Such an one stumbleth not, for he seeth the daylight around him:
If a man walk in the night, he stumbleth on in his blindness,
There is no light in him, and this is the cause that he stumbleth.
Our friend Lazarus sleepeth, but I must go to awake him."

" Lord, if he sleep it is well: for hard is the path of the wayworn:
Stones and thorns lie around it, and wearily children of Adam
Turn from the labors of life with its care, with its toil, with its
    sorrow,
When the bright Angel of God takes post for the night by their
    pillow."

" Lazarus sleepeth in death, and we must go and behold him,
I for your sakes am glad that I was not there when he slum-
    bered—
Now will I stablish your faith."

        'Twas thus in mystical warning
Spake the Christ with His own as they gazed on the stream of
    the Jordan.
They understood Him not as He stood on the verge of His Passion,
Waiting till death should weave the crown of thorns for His
    garland,
Crown which shall bud with the blossoms of life in the valley of
    Hades,
E'en in the realms of Death, when Death himself is defeated.

They understood Him not. Full well the soul of the Saviour
Saw before Him the shades of Gethsemane; saw the full chalice
Which he must drink alone, ere they could know that in Jesus
Death is the gate of Life, the passage to joys immortal.

"Lazarus sleepeth.   I go to awake him."   Child of the Virgin,
Speak to us then!   Ah, speak to us thus, when we too shall
    slumber
After the fever of life in the grave of peaceful awaiting.

"I am the Resurrection, and I am the Life for believers;
Whoso believeth in Me, although he were dead, yet he liveth.
Death hath no more dominion o'er him that liveth in Jesus."
Thus as the years roll on, the voice of the priest in the church-
    yard
Sweetly greets the departed who come to rest in its bosom,
Bosom pregnant with life—Seed-land for the Lord of the harvest,
When He shall send His Angels to bear the sheaves to His
    garner.

"I am the Resurrection, and I am the Life for believers:"
Spake the sweet voice of the Christ, as He stood by the grave of
    the loved one,
He slept calm and still, and his soul was gone to the mansion
Where the departed await the trumpet-call to the Judgment.
Silent and undisturbed he roamed through the ivory moonlight,
Bathing in light the dim meadows of Asphodel; far in the dis-
    tance
Saw he the shadowy forms of the patriarch fathers of Hades,
Wearily waiting the summons of Him who cometh in triumph,
Breaking the brazen gates and their bars of iron asunder.

Hark! 'tis the voice of the Master!   He calleth thee!   Soul of the
    sleeper,
Thee alone doth He call—Come forth!   Come forth!   He com-
    mands thee:
"Lazarus, come thou forth!"

He feels the grave-clothes around him,
Swathing yet once more the form of his earthly corruption,
As his obedient spirit reënters the clay of the body.

"Lazarus, come thou forth! thou must sup with me ere my passion:
Life and death must sit down together at Bethany. Think not
Thy life's work complete, nor that death again can fold thee
Ere thou hast stood in the darkness beneath the Cross of thy
    Saviour,
Guiding the souls of the recognized dead when the grave shall
    return to them
Here to receive the blessing which quick and dead must inherit
Under the outspread arms, the bleeding hands of Atonement."

GERARD MOULTRIE.

FROM THE ARABIC.

He who died at Azim sends
This to comfort all his friends:

Faithful friends! It lies, I know,
Pale and white and cold as snow,
And ye say, "Abdullah's dead!
Weeping at the feet and head.
I can see your falling tears;
I can hear your sighs and prayers;
Yet I smile and whisper this,
"I am not the thing you kiss.
Cease your tears, and let it lie,
It *was* mine, it is not I."

Sweet friends! what the women lave
For the last sleep of the grave,
Is a hut which I am quitting,
Is a garment no more fitting,
Is a cage, from which, at last,
Like a bird, my soul hath pass'd.
Love the inmate, not the room,
The wearer, not the garb; the plume
Of the eagle, not the bars
That kept him from those splendid stars.

Loving friends! be wise, and dry
Straightway every weeping eye.
What ye lift upon the bier
Is not worth a single tear.
'Tis an empty sea-shell, one
Out of which the pearl is gone;
The shell is broken, it lies there;
The pearl, the all, the soul, is here.
'Tis an earthen jar, whose lid
Allah seal'd, the while it hid
That treasure of his treasury,
A mind that loved him: let it lie.
Let the shards be earth once more,
Since the gold is in his store.

Allah glorious! Allah good!
Now Thy world is understood;
Now the long, long wonder ends;
Yet ye weep, my foolish friends,
While the man whom ye *call* dead,
In unspoken bliss, instead,

Lives and loves you; lost, 'tis true,
For the light that shines for you.
But in the light ye cannot see
Of undisturb'd felicity—
In a perfect Paradise,
And a life that never dies.

Farewell, friends! but *not* farewell;
Where I am, ye too shall dwell.
I am gone before your face,
A moment's worth, a little space.
When ye come where I have stepp'd,
Ye will wonder why ye wept.
Ye will know, by true love taught,
That *here* is all, and there is naught;
Weep awhile, if ye are fain;
Sunshine still must follow rain;
Only not at Death, for Death,
Now we know, is that first breath
Which our souls draw when we enter
Life, which is of all life centre.

Be ye certain, all seems love.
View'd from Allah's throne above.
Be ye stout of heart, and come
Bravely onward to your home.
La-il Allah—Allah la,
O Love divine, O Love alway.

He who died at Azim gave
This to those who made his grave.

FIFTH WEDNESDAY.

THE LAMB OF GOD.

St. John the Baptist knew him not, but was warned by the One who sent him, that upon whomsoever he should see the spirit descending and remaining on Him, "the same is He which baptizeth with the Holy Ghost." Perhaps many others were receiving Baptism that same day—and among the crowd—the Baptist, prophet as he was, could discern no difference. The great teacher, of whom all men spoke, came among the rest. But St. John could not have known of His Divinity, though he said "I have need to be baptized of Thee and comest Thou to me"—for St. John the Evangelist records, "I knew Him not." He must have felt, "Here is one greater than I am," but till he saw the heavens opened, he could not have known the whole revelation of God. But he had long watched for the mystic sign, which was to follow the Baptism of the Son of Man; with what a thrill he must have seen the strange Dove

descending out of the Heavens, and the voice —
the voice of God Himself. What high thoughts
this should give us of Baptism. What if we
should see what every day perhaps the angels see,
the mysterious Dove descending on some baby's
head — as the mystic water is poured upon it.
That was the first Christian Baptism. Do we
know that the same descent does not always take
place—only that our eyes are holden? That the
heavenly part of that initial Baptism is not always, *always* carried out? O the weight of this
body! the darkening, blinding eyes that think they
see, the impotent brain that thinks it thinks,
while it is only hindering thought! The rush,
the thrill, the ecstasy when spirit is free; and the
dead thing is left behind.

———

Ye would not sit at ease while meek men kneel
Did ye but see His face shine through the veil,
And the unearthly forms that round you steal
Hidden in beauteous light, splendent or pale
As the rich Service leads. And prostrate faith
Shroudeth her timorous eye, while through the air
Hovers and hangs the Spirit's cleansing Breath
In Whitsun shapes o'er each true worshipper.

Deep wreaths of Angels, burning from the East,
Around the consecrated Shrine are braced,
The awful Stone where by fit hands are placed
The Flesh and Blood of the tremendous Feast.
But kneel—the priest upon the Altar-stair
Will bring a blessing out of Sion there.

F. W. FABER.

FIFTH THURSDAY.

IF one were to go every day to the habitation of His house, the "place where His honor dwelleth," where two or three are gathered together in His name; and in sincerity and simplicity make this prayer, would it not be a sure safeguard against sin? Hedged in by all those promises and covenants, how could it be otherwise? If we were not wanting in our part, there can be no doubt, a life so guarded would be one of comparative innocence. Not one free from temptations, and errors, and repentances, but one that might bear the name of righteousness. O how much lies within our reach that we do not put out our hands and take! What power over evil spirits, over our own spirits, over God Himself by His own mercy—we have placed before us in prayer. And how wily and how wise our enemy is, at the very outset to dull that weapon, and make us hate our prayers; weary of them, faithless about them,

(165)

sometimes neglectful of them altogether.   One rarely says a prayer without a temptation to some sin
about it.   But if we persevere through all discour-
agements, the prayer will reach Heaven through all
hindrances.   About this daily repeated form of supplication it is good to remember how many thousands are saying it for this one day; how sanctified
it must be by all these many devout lips; how strong
a front we make against the Evil One by such agreement of desire.   It is good to be encouraged by it,
to remember that it is possible for us to be kept
without deadly sin; and that such should be our
aim.   And beyond all else we should learn always
to pray and not to faint; daily to pray and not
to look forward — only to look at the day's sins,
and guard against them, and pray against them.
Being so mortal and so finite we can deal best
with each day by itself, leaving the past, and the
future, to the One into whose hands the first has
passed, and who still holds the last.

———

Be not afraid to pray—to pray is right;
Pray if thou canst with hope; but ever pray
Though hope be weak or sick with long delay;

Pray in the darkness if there be no light.
Far is the time remote from human sight
When war and discord on the earth shall cease;
Yet every prayer for universal peace
Avails, the blessed time to expedite.
Whate'er is good to wish, ask that of Heaven
Though it be what thou canst not hope to see.
Pray to be perfect, though material leaven
Forbid the spirit, so, on earth to be;
But if for any wish thou canst not pray,
Then pray to God to cast that wish away!

HARTLEY COLERIDGE.

FIFTH FRIDAY.

Mary's Thank-offering.—St. John, xii. 1 to 10.

What a different scene, in the home at Bethany!
A supper, at which are many guests, some come
from love, and to rejoice, no doubt; others, not for
Jesus' sake only, but that they might see Lazarus
also, whom He had raised from the dead. And
Lazarus himself sits at the table with Him; as a
guest, a traveller, a stranger returned from that unknown land, to which none of them have ever been.
We can think with what wonder and awe they
looked upon him, second only to that with which
they regarded The One who had had power to call
him back. We can scarcely believe it possible
that we could sit quietly at a table where such
strange guests were met. They must have known
that they were in the presence of God; and there
before them sat, one who had *died* and was alive
again; one who had lain in the grave four days, one
whom with their own eyes they had seen come forth,
bound hand and foot with grave-clothes. Of all this

(168)

there was, there could be, no doubt, and yet they sat there quietly, and ate and drank; and one of His own disciples could find the hardihood to say, why, at this high moment, and in this high presence, why was this ointment used for *this*?

It would be wise, perhaps, for us to remember that it is possible for us to become used to the sight and thought of what should always fill us with awe. And that it is a snare of our human nature to do so; and one of the temptations of our mortal state. But no familiarity could make the thought commonplace and trite to Mary. She feels to her heart's core the reverential awe and love that is due to One who is the God of all the world, and yet her personal and tender friend. He is the resurrection and the life: He is her brother's life and resurrection. She is in the presence of all the Glory of Heaven, though veiled and hidden: and she remembers the glory while only the veil meets her eye. How acceptable this is to her Lord! He cares what His creatures think of Him. He would be worshipped with holy worship. He is jealous of His honor.

This act of thanksgiving and worship; this offering of what was costly and princely called forth His special praise. No specious pretence of benefit to the human family can ever after this stand in the way of offerings to God, as God, one would think. Render unto God, the things that are God's. Build your temples, make beautiful your worship: then go and serve your brother on your knees, with your substance, with your sympathy, with the labor of your hands. But do not put the one for the other, in any case. Do not believe you will be acquitted for neglect of one by fulfilment of the other. This should ye have done and not have left the other undone. God's laws to the Jews about their worship should teach us something. And the world is not so very much older now. Men are not so very much more spiritual. They need much the same things as they needed then, in general laws. If we love God whom we have not seen, enough to worship Him truly, we cannot help loving our brother whom we have seen, enough to serve him earnestly, affectionately, self-denyingly.

"I will not offer burnt offerings without cost."

"Why deck the high cathedral roof
With foliage rich and rare,
With crowns and flowerets far aloft,
To none but angels fair?

Why for the lofty altar hide
  Thy gems and gold in store?
Why spread the burnished pall so wide
  Upon the chancel floor?"

Nay, rather ask, why duteous boy
  And mother-loving maid,
Scarce in their filial gifts find joy,
  If nought of theirs be paid;

Why hearts, that true love tokens need,
  For brother or for friend
Count not the cost with careful heed,
  But haste their all to spend.

Ask why of old the favored King
  Inquired the Temple's price
Not bearing to his Lord to bring
  An unbought sacrifice.

Yea, lowly fall, and of thy Lord
  In silence ask, and dread:
Why praised He Mary's ointment poured
  Upon His sacred head.

                                KEBLE.

O Jesu, Pierced for love of me,
How can this poor heart grateful be?
Would that my burning love might be
Even as is Thy Love to me.

Now on a wonderous wise dost Thou
Thy very self on me bestow:
Love bids Thee stoop to be so low—
But who that depth of Love can know?

Oh! come to me dear Lord I pray,
And let Thy Love my spirit stay:
Behold, it longeth sore for Thee,
I would it might more worthy be.
To Forest streams the Hart doth hie,
When he for thirst is fain to die;
And so my soul doth pant for Thee,
O Jesu, Jesu, come to me.

I cannot love Thee as I would,
Yet pardon me, O Highest Good;
My life, and all I call mine own,
I lay before Thine Altar-Throne:
And if a thousand lives were mine,
O sweetest Lord, they should be Thine;
And scanty would the offering be,
So richly hast thou loved me.

SISTER M.

FIFTH SATURDAY.

GOD is offended by this state of mind: it is an affront to Him, doubting His infinite power to keep His word and guard His child. I do not cease to love perhaps, but I cease to believe. I ought to have desponded long ago indeed, poor atom, if I had depended on myself. God is the same that He was before I believed: yesterday, to-day, and forever able to perform all my petitions—pledged to perform them if they are in accord with truth and purity and piety. Men ought always to pray and not to faint—what right have I to faint? That is the work of the enemy; I must remember to recognize it. When I most despond, I must most pray and hold to my external religious acts most tenaciously, Despondency is a temptation which is very subtile, because it seems so entirely involuntary—it comes—it cannot be got rid of. So be it. I cannot make myself buoyant when my heart is like lead. I cannot see heaven when I feel as if I were buried under clods of earth—I cannot compose Te Deums when I am weeping a De Profundis. But this I can do. I can hold me fast by God—and make Him my refuge until this tyranny be overpast. I can take with me words and come into His presence. I can strengthen my memory by His promises though I cannot feel them. I can despise feelings and count only facts. I can be patient if I cannot be hopeful. It is a temptation, and not a sin, to be sad, to be in heaviness. But it is a sin to rest in such a state without earnest effort to escape from it. Such a state is full of danger— it leads to the most fearful issues that we can contemplate as far as our mortal life is concerned. It is perilous in all its stages, paralyzing, benumbing. It is only by prayers—which I can read if I cannot say (God knows the intention of my heart), by acts of love to others and resolutely going on in outward duties, whether I feel inclined for them or not, that I can hope to conquer this temptation of the malicious enemy. Even if he triumphs over me to the end (which God in His mercy forbid to be), there is a world in which he has no power, and *in which I have a part.*

"As thy days, so shall thy strength be."—Deut. xxxiii.
"Trust ye in the Lord forever: for in the Lord Jehovah everlasting strength."—Isa. xxvi. 4

O fellow Christian! whosoe'er thou art,
    This is for thee and me—
This wine of Trust that maketh glad the heart
    In its adversity:
Drink, therefore, and so bear a braver part;
    For as thy days, thy strength shall be.

"Thy days" may be a dull and vacant range,
    A long captivity,
Nought brightly wonderful or sweetly strange
    To quicken time for thee:
Less pain or more the only interchange;
    Yet as thy days, thy strength shall be.

"Thy days" may be a long experience
    Of much perplexity:
The light it longs for, amid clouds so dense
    Thy mind may scarcely see:
Then on thy Father cast thy confidence;
    And as thy days, thy strength shall be.

O burdened sufferer in a world of woe,
    Thy sorrow's mystery
Shall pass: *believe*, and one day thou shalt *know;*
    Above thine eyes shall see,
Be not impatient of the veil *below*,
    And as thy days, thy strength shall be.

Amen! until there shall be no more "days,"
    Until the shadows flee,

Until the cloud be lifted from our gaze
   Until in certainty
Trust die, and Faith in Sight, and Prayer in Praise,
  In GOD'S ETERNITY!

S. J. STONE.

" Those fervent raptures are forever flown:
And, since their date, my soul hath undergone
Change manifold, for better or for worse:
Yet cease I not to struggle, and aspire
Heavenward; and chide the part of me that flags,
Through sinful choice; or dread necessity,
On human Nature from above imposed.
'Tis by comparison, an easy task
Earth to despise; but, to converse with Heaven—
This is not easy: to relinquish all
We have, or hope, of happiness and joy,
And stand in freedom loosened from this world,
I deem not arduous:—but must needs confess
That 'tis a thing impossible to frame
Conceptions equal to the soul's desires;
And the most difficult of tasks to *keep*
Heights which the soul is competent to gain.
—Man is of dust: ethereal hopes are his,
Which when they should sustain themselves aloft,
Want due consistence; like a pillar of smoke,
That with majestic energy from earth
Rises; but having reached the thinner air,
Melts, and dissolves, and is no longer seen.
From this infirmity of mortal kind

Sorrow proceeds, which else were not;—at least,
If Grief be something hallowed and ordained,
If, in proportion, it be just and meet,
Through this, 'tis able to maintain its hold,
In that excess which Conscience disapproves.
For who could sink and settle to that point
Of selfishness; so senseless who could be
As long and perseveringly to mourn
For any object of his love, removed
From this unstable world, if he could fix
A satisfying view upon that state
Of pure imperishable blessedness,
Which reason promises, and Holy Writ
Insures to all Believers? Yet mistrust
Is of such incapacity, methinks,
No natural branch; despondency far less.
And, if there be whose tender frames have drooped
Even to the dust; apparently through weight
Of anguish unrelieved, and lack of power
An agonizing sorrow to transmute,
Infer not hence a hope from those withheld
When wanted most; a confidence impaired
So pitiably, that having ceased to see
With bodily eyes, they are borne down by love
Of what is lost, and perish through regret.
Oh! no, full oft the innocent sufferer sees
Too clearly; feels too vividly; and longs
To realize the Vision, with intense
And over-constant yearning—there—there lies
The excess, by which the balance is destroyed.

12

Too, too contracted are these walls of flesh,
This vital warmth too cold, these visual orbs,
Though inconceivably endowed, too dim
For any passion of the soul that leads
To ecstasy: and, all the crooked paths
Of time and change disdaining, takes its course
Along the line of limitless desires.
I, speaking now from such disorder free,
Nor rapt, nor craving, but in settled peace,
I cannot doubt that They whom you deplore
Are glorified ; or, if they sleep, shall wake
From sleep, and dwell with God in endless love.
Hope, below this, consists not with belief
In mercy, carried infinite degrees
Beyond the tenderness of human hearts :
Hope, below this, consists not with belief
In perfect Wisdom, guiding mightiest Power,
That finds no limits but her own pure Will.

WILLIAM WORDSWORTH.

FIFTH SUNDAY.

THE new life is begun in Baptism, is renewed by prayer, by penitence, by the Holy Eucharist. It is an entirely different life from the natural life—so opposed to it that we must never be surprised at its incongruity. We must accept, that it leads us into different rooms, that it requires of us different duties. It is this trying to lead the two lives that makes such poor meagre service, forms such weak Christians. We ask to be holy as He is holy, while we try to match our pace with those who are marching to the world's music. Oh! what is the use! *Ye cannot serve God and mammon*—God knows best about us, having made us, and He says that we *cannot*, not that we had better not, nor should not, but that we *cannot*. Why not accept it and choose this day whom we will serve. There is pleasure enough in the new life; there is profit enough; there is *safety*—"Mortify your members which are upon

(179)

the earth." A hard lesson. Rise to the new life; don't fall back into the old. And oh! the heights, the blisses that await us! Not in a day—not in a Lent—but in a life of whatever years God pleases. The new life is trial, mortification, dissent from companions, is patience, humility, self-contempt,— in that body that now is; but in the body that shall be—joy, peace, companionship with angels, triumph and utter satisfaction. God! are we beings of immortal destiny—have we a spark of Thy Divinity dwelling in us, and do we hesitate a moment in our choice; do we waver to whom we shall go? Lord thou hast the words of eternal life. We go to Thee. We rise with Thee out of the grave of our past life. We accept Thy will and we will to die to the sinful world and to glorify Thee as Thou shalt lead us.

Yes, thou forgivest, but with all forgiving
    canst not renew mine innocence again:
Make Thou, O Christ, a dying of my living,
    purge from the sin but never from the pain!

So shall all speech of now and of to-morrow,
    all He hath shown me or shall show me yet,
Spring from an infinite and tender sorrow,
    burst from a burning passion of regret.

F. W. H. MYERS.

"Severe the life that fits for God
One day the Thorns; one day the Rod;
Ever on bleeding back, the Cross—
Ever the Fire to burn the Dross.

Smoothly along we cannot sail,
One day the Calm; one day the Gale;
Ever the Rocks on either side
Ever the Prow against the tide.

Shorter the Life, by every breath;
One day Disease and one day Death—
Ever the falling shades of night
Ever the Grave in open sight.

Nearer the Port by every wave,
Be strong my soul, my heart be brave—
Theirs is the gain who suffer loss
Theirs is the Crown, who bear the Cross."

A. M.

FIFTH MONDAY.

———◆———

THE VOICE FROM HEAVEN.

" THIS is my beloved Son in whom I am well pleased." It must have been music to the ears of our dear, exiled Lord, these words from home. How long He had listened to our poor tongue; how patiently He had borne the clamor of earth! I can not remember any other heavenly voices—except the angels' song at His birth—and the voice, just before the Passion in answer to the prayer, "Father, glorify Thy name"—and the angel's who ministered to Him in His Agony. All this time the language of Heaven had been perhaps unheard by Him. He who "felt all that He might pity all" perhaps knew once the sorrow of homesickness.

When does the voice from Heaven sound for our welcome? Always perhaps at our Baptism. For then surely Our Father is well pleased, even in us. When we are for that first moment, freed from sin, fresh from the laver of regeneration,—when the mor-

(182)

tal stain is washed away, and we are as never before,—as never after, in the flesh, *pure*. O then,
at that moment, perhaps the voice sounds, though
we do not hear it—and God is well pleased. And
once again, we know—we are to hope to hear the
voice of commendation from the Throne of power,
" Well done, good and faithful servant : enter thou
into the joy of thy Lord." Ah ! what a different moment from that in which the praise of our Baptismal
purity was spoken. O the long road of falling, sinning, repenting, battling, praying, that lays between
the child's unheard benediction, and the saint's hard
won blessing. Those words will pay for all. Can I
not see the tired, bruised, only-not-fainting soul,
fallen prostrate at the feet of Christ ; while the
music of those words fill every sense—while their
sweetness and glory flow over all the hard and cruel
past—soothe and comfort every wound—make an
eternity of bliss of that one moment.

———

Safe home, Safe home in port!
—Rent cordage, shattered deck,
Torn sails, provisions short,
And only not a wreck :

But oh! the joy upon the shore
To tell our voyage-perils o'er!

The prize, the prize secure!
The athlete nearly fell;
Bare all he *could* endure
And bare not always well:
But he may smile at troubles gone
Who sets the victor-garland on!

No more the foe can harm ;
No more of leaguer'd camp,
And cry of night alarm
And need of ready lamp :
And yet how nearly he had failed,—
How nearly had that foe prevailed!

The lamb is in the fold
In perfect safety penn'd:
The lion once had hold
And thought to make an end:
But One came by with Wounded side,
And for the sheep the Shepherd died.

The exile is at home!
—O nights and days of tears,
O longings not to roam,
O sins and doubt and fears.—
What matter now (when so men say)
The King has wiped those tears away?

O happy, happy Bride!
Thy widow'd hours are past,
The bridegroom at thy side,
Thou all His own at last!
The sorrows of thy former cup
In full fruition swallowed up!

                                    J. M. NEALE.

FIFTH TUESDAY.

LET us think awhile of the influences of Prayer in the education of the Soul.

God is jealous over the soul, which He has created for Himself. He will educate His Own Child. It is His pleasure to communicate His mind in secret to the soul He loves. "Surely the Lord God will do nothing but He revealeth His secret unto His servants the prophets." And the instrument of this Divine intelligence is prayer. He may send ministers to sow the seed and Angels or shepherds to kindle the spark; but it is by keeping their sayings and pondering them in their heart (and this is one action of prayer) that the Saint's life is formed upon the mind of God. Also by reserving to Himself the communication of this knowledge, God proves to us the dignity and capacity of the soul. He will not suffer it to be content with any Teacher but Himself. When Jesus draws Mary to sit at His feet, He proves not only his willingness to teach, but that He has ennobled her with the ability to learn.

By the same exercise of prayer He draws out
the affections to Himself. He invites our familiar
presence. He makes us His friends. "Frequent
devotion maintains this friendship with God ;" and
He is ever more ready to hear than we to pray. In
social life we know how many friends of youth are
lost by our correspondence failing. The love may
abide, but the liking is less. The community of interest declines, sympathy is less quick. Oh, think
what life gains by prayer which cherishes in us a
a "hearty liking to God."

Again, we know the value of the inheritance of
a name, whose noble life has bequeathed to us great
interests ; and the richer blessing of a living friend,
whose calm wisdom and wide knowledge and pure
sympathy saves us from sinking in the menial service of the world. Well, and what does prayer do ?
Does it not bind us to the generations of all Saints
and all heroic Christian lives, and lay down lines
beneath the grave by which from our earthly homes
we communicate our sympathies to and fro with
souls in Paradise ? "All the good men from the
beginning of time to this hour have practised prayer.
Not one of them now in a better world, but practised it." And so writes Bishop Wilson also in

acknowledgment of the scope of prayer, its dominion in the spiritual world, and the difficulty of ac-
quiring the habit of it. "He that has learned to
pray as he ought, has got the secret of a holy life."

Again, prayer, it may be said, immediately con-
nects us with all those homes of piety, where the
hidden life of men of God is attracting grace, as
mountain tops draw clouds, and is storing up a
wealth of treasure, as Joseph in his wise economy
stored up beforehand seven years' harvest against
seven years of famine. Oh, if we would believe, that
the whole world were richer by reason even of a few
living a life of prayer: that the weary days of the
invalid, the offerings of the priest, the fastings of
the penitent, if in their appointed lot they under-
take the secret ministry of prayer, not only hallow
their Father's holy Name, but make His Kingdom
come upon the earth, as truly as the Apostle, who
creates new churches, and the Evangelist, who by
his preaching of the Gospel makes the dry bones to
gather flesh and live !

In the Kingdom of Christ there is need of S.
John, who shall lie on the Bosom of His Lord, as
there is need of S. Peter, who shall step out first in
front to confess the truth, and walk on the water to

go to Jesus, and judge the hypocrite, whose lying
heart is bringing confusion into the Church. The
men of action cannot do their work, unless there be
men of prayer beside them to communicate with the
inner mind of Christ. Why did S. Peter bid S. John
to inquire of the Lord, who it was that should betray
Him, but for the consciousness that S. John was
living closer to the hidden life of the Son of God?
In the same way Martha could not satisfy her Lord
by the utmost of her active ministries upon Him,
unless Mary sat at His Feet in quiet contemplation,
and in the attitude of a reverent listening to His
thoughts. The Church not only requires prayer to
be offered in its own place, but cannot do her active
work without the help of men of prayer. And,
again, it is to be insisted on, that, while the distinc-
tion between the active and contemplative life is to
be recognized, they shall not be divorced from one
another. "What God hath joined together, let no
man put asunder." No man can be Christ-like, who
does not combine in fair proportions both characters.
If one side of his life exhibit S. Peter, the other
must express S. John.

Again, consider how the exercise of prayer in-
creases charity—charity which makes us in respect

to others patient and liberal. By prayer we extend our interests in the loftiest things of man and God: we promote cheerfulness and banish dullness from our hearts. Now, whereas dullness in ourselves provokes impatience and bitterness toward others (while we resent on them the stinging provocations of our own disquietude), an access of fresh interests infers an increase of hopefulness, and so we look on the world around us with a brighter eye. "We know that all things work together for good to them that love God." We know it if we are used to pray! The surface of human life is strewn with ills enough to vex every soul that has a thought for righteousness. Beneath the crust is treasure, it may be the dust of bodies that will rise to eternal life. Everywhere "good is undermost;" but the divining rod is prayer. Rev. C. W. Furse.

"The Master saith, My time is at hand."—St. Matt. xxvi. 18.

"The spirit indeed is willing, but the flesh is weak."—St. Matt. xxvi. 41.

Soon will the Holy Week be here;
It is as if my Lord were near,
And, half in hope and half in fear,

I went to meet Him, so to be
A witness of the agony
And bitter passion borne for me.

"In hope" that so my soul may gain
Harvest of joy from seeds of pain;
That, flooding over heart and brain,

A deeper sense of sinful night
May drive me closer to the Light
To read His Love with clearer sight.

"In fear" lest even while I weep,
As once of old forgetful sleep
Should o'er the 'willing spirit' creep,

And I should hear, as heard the Three,
Those words of chiding sympathy,
"Couldst thou not watch one hour with Me?"

Be Hope the stronger! O be Thou,
Dear Lord, the Guardian of my vow
To keep my vigil near Thee now:

Aid my "weak flesh" this holy tide,
That I, despite or sloth or pride,
May watch and pray as at Thy side. Amen.

S. J. STONE.

SIXTH WEDNESDAY.

———◆———

St. John, xvi. 5.

THE unknown; that is the most subtle, most profound form of awe. Truly, in the parting at death, how much of our pain might be appeased, if we knew whither they went, from whom we parted. If one word might come back to us from them, if we might look one moment upon the actual life they are gone to live, it would take away, it seems, half the load upon our hearts. Yes, truly, it is awful, that parting; how human nature lives through the sundering of ties so close and vital, is as amazing as that it lives at all. In a moment, all is dark; there is an end; there is no voice nor any to answer. There is a silence, forever, till the darkness opens to swallow us up too. "Sorrow hath filled your hearts." Ah, what else could fill them! It is a mercy, if not mad despair. Now, considering the sharp defining separation between the life of the body on earth, and

(192)

the life of the spirit in the world beyond; what does it behoove a Christian to do, to prepare for the moment when he shall look into the darkening eyes of the one he loves best and say "whither goest thou?" Or for the moment when the pains of death have taken hold upon him, and the horrible dread of the unknown have overwhelmed him? Is it by forgetting that that day is coming? Is it by living filled and satisfied by the present life? Or is it by daily praying for strength in the coming trial; by throwing our thoughts ahead into the life without the body; by lighting that lamp of faith, which alone can keep us from frantic terror in the darkness? *For there is nothing else;* no one has ever found another light that would live in that gloom; and hundreds of thousands have found that, and found it light enough. There is no use in speculating and turning our *minds* to this; we must turn our souls to it, and pray, and believe, and trust that His strength shall be made perfect in our weakness, when the day of our great weakness comes. There is no danger of dwelling too much on this, if we are in ordinary life—all abstracting of the mind from temporal sight is elevating, and nature will

13

not suffer from this contradiction. Let it be our
daily prayer, to be succored in the day of trial;
our daily thought, the life of the soul separated
from the body; our daily effort, to love more the
things of God, and less the things of sense. To
judge righteous judgment between them; in little
practical commonplace questions, to decide in favor of unseen things. To put the life of the soul
first. To live, in little details, with the thought
of that "whither" before us. Not to be discour-
aged with the littleness of sacrifices and efforts to
live a holy life. To remember that great journeys
are walked in single steps, which seem very tire-
some as they are made. To enlighten our minds
about eternity, we must darken them about earth.
There is no danger of too great indifference to the
present; the world, and the flesh, and the devil, are
as yet too strong for that.

———

At noon-tide came a voice "Thou must away;
Hast thou some look to give, some word to say,
Or hear, of fond farewell," I answered, "Nay,

My soul hath said its farewell long ago.
How light, when Summer comes, the loosened snow,
Slides from the hills! yet tell me, *where I go*,

Doth any wait for me?" Then like the clear
Full drops of summer rain that seem to cheer
The skies they fall from, soft within mine ear,

And slow, as if to render through that sweet
Delay a blest assurance more complete,
"Yea," only "yea," was whisper'd me, and then
A silence that was unto it, Amen.

"Doth any love me'there," I said, "or mark
Within the dull, cold flint the fiery spark
One moment flashing out into the dark?

"My spirit glow'd, yet burn'd not to a clear,
Warm, steadfast flame, to lighten or to cheer;"
The sweet voice said, "By things which do appear

We judge amiss. The flower which wears its way
Through stony chinks, lives on from day to day,
Approved for living let the rest be gay

And sweet as Summer! Heaven within the reed
Lists for the flute-note, in the folded seed
It sees the bud, and in the Will the Deed."

DORA GREENWELL.

Yea, though I walk through the Valley of the Shadow of Death, I will fear no evil; for Thou art with me, Thy Rod and Thy Staff comfort me.

———

When day's shadows lengthen,
　Jesu, be Thou near;
Pardon, comfort, strengthen,
　Chase away my fear;
Love and Hope be deepened,
　Faith more strong and clear.

When the night grows darkest,
　And the stars are pale,
When the foe assembles
　In Death's misty vale,
Be Thou Sword and Helmet,
　Be Thou Shield and Mail.

He, who stands beside me,
　Comes but to proclaim
Pardon for contrition,
　Wipes out stains of shame,
Saying—I absolve thee
　In Christ's blessed Name.

If Thou willest, feed me,
　Strengthen, ere I go;
In that unknown pathway
　Lighten every woe;
JESU, as Thou knowest,
　Grant me so to know.

That an hour of weakness—
    That a time of fear—
Come, Thou Bread of Heaven,
    Sacrament so dear;
All I love may vanish
    If but Thou be near.

Come, Thou Food of Angels,
    Source of every grace,
In Thy Father's Mansions
    Give me soon a place,
That unveiled in Splendor
    I may see Thy Face.

Fading this world, fading,
    Forms are growing dim,
Other voices whisper
    Tones of some sweet hymn,
Telling of His Mercy,
    Speaking but of Him.

By the Jordan's ripples,
    Passing through the shade;
Let me hear that promise
    Once for ever made—
It is I, Thy JESUS;
    Be not thou afraid.

Cold the waters rolling,
    Chill the mists around,
Black the night above me,
    Strange th' untrodden ground,

Oft lost in the desert,
   Yet may I be found.

Then be near me, JESUS,
   Enemies shall flee;
Ave, Sacramentum,
   Thou my Comfort be,
Food, and Priest, and Victim,
   Let me feed on Thee.

So shall no fears chill me
   On that unknown shore,
For in death He conquered
   And can die no more;
His hand guards and guides me
   To the City's door.

Blessed warfare over,
   Endless Rest alone,
Tears no more, nor sorrow,
   Neither sigh nor moan,
But a song of triumph
   Round about the Throne.

                            F. G. LEE.

SIXTH THURSDAY.

THE TWO GREAT COMMANDMENTS.

FIRST.

AND His commandments are not grievous. The first, Love. The second, Love. And on these two hang all the Law and the Prophets. No one ought to complain of such a service as that. Truly if we could get our hearts right it would be easy enough. It is the perpetual struggle of the part of us that has not come under the yoke of Christ, to regain the rest, that gives Satan all his power, and weakens us so sadly. If we were *utterly* consecrated, unreservedly given up to God to the very core of the heart, how easy would it be to keep those two commandments. If we loved God beyond all else, nothing would seem hard ; everything would have a buoyant brightness and delight ; we could not be made to suffer. It is easy to imagine a state of mind that would render earthly trials perfectly insignificant ; recall the few moments in one's own life in which that Love

(199)

seemed supreme; then intensify it by continual possession, and imagine it spread over the whole life, growing in daily strength. What would earthly trial effect on such a spirit? But alas! This is only ideal. Can it ever be anything else? Has God set any bounds to purely spiritual petitions? Have we a right to ask for such a love? Has any one ever sought for it, ever fought for it, as for life, through many years, and been denied it? Do we set our aim high enough? Are we not satisfied to be *just saved?* Is it God's will that we should go halting, faint-hearted through our whole journey? Is it God's will, or our own want of will?

These are the things that always seem to stand in the way. Temperament, Timidity, Frivolity. Temperament seems the greatest, most opposing, most material objection. How can persons who are dull, easily depressed, unecstatic, not naturally yielding to the force of emotions, give themselves up to, and keep themselves under the control of that which is purely of the emotions, which is an invisible, spiritual power! If earthly love does not fill them with constant rapture, how can that which is unseen, fill them with constant purpose and content? Can one fight against one's nature, and gain this power? Would the passionate longing and desire for it, and steady asking for it, not win *at least* the tender compassion and personal affection of our dear Lord?

Again, We are afraid to ask for the highest places, because we know that great graces come through suffering. We dare not ask that we "may love Him as well as ever any creature loved Him," because we fear that that may make it necessary that we suffer as much as any of His saints ever suffered. But *is* that necessary; He does not love to afflict us, and if we can gain those promises, may He not spare us some of the dreadful things that are so revolting to flesh and blood. At least we may remember that of all the Twelve, S. John, the one He loved, the one who loved Him best, was never called to the death of martyrdom. Of course we must be willing to pay whatever price He asks for the seat at His right hand; but we must remember, if we are solely relying on Him, He can make all the cruel pains endurable, and He does, and has made them so hundreds of times that we may read of, and hear of, and see.

Then, we are so frivolous and it is so hard to

keep ever in mind that which can only be *in mind,* and which concerns the spirit only. It is easy to wish it and to pray it once. But it is so hard to make it the intention of our lives, and the rule of our conduct. Would not this be well? To link our days together by *one* earnest ardent daily prayer for grace to keep the first and great commandment. To *mean it* just as simply and matter-of-factly as we would mean to take a journey or to read a book. To keep meaning it and repeating it, without discouragement — to pray passionately and earnestly whenever we can; to pray determinedly and patiently whenever we cannot pray in any better way. *Always to pray and not to faint.*

"OUT OF THE DEEP."

Fain is the wakened soul to try
Her pinions in the golden sky
Of peace and pardon instantly:

But they are clogged by thoughts that fill
Her mind with memories of ill,
A worldly love, a carnal will.

And she is forced to sit and weep,
And watch alone in valleys deep
The darker shadows onward creep.

As though to whelm her in a tomb
Of utter spiritual gloom,
Foretaste of the eternal doom.

"My sin!" the low despairing sigh;
"My sin!" the exceeding bitter cry,
Out of those depths is heard on high:

Glad angels hear it where they stand,
And wait, a ministering band—
Their Lord's permission and command:

It comes—and swiftly, down from heaven
A light whereby that gloom is riven!
A voice of power and peace, "Forgiven!"

O blessed voice! O living light!
To wake those silent depths, and smite
With beams of day the vale of night.

But ah! not yet is peace complete,
The foemen fiercer for defeat,
Strive to regain their ancient seat.

The world, forsaken, brings again
Its joys and cares; the will would fain
Its realm recover and retain.

And though that Light still shineth clear
Through those new shades, and though the ear
Hears still that Voice it loves to hear,

Speak, as of old, on Galilee,
"Peace:" yet withal, the heart must see
And hate its own infirmity:

And cries, as one who cries for breath,
Worn and oppressed, " I faint beneath
The alien body of this death ! "

'Tis well, for otherwise than so,
The soul, disdaining to lie low,
A deeper depth of ill might know.

A darker gloom, a gulf more wide,
Because a self-exalting pride
Would thrust her farther from His side.

Therefore the Church, that she may lead
Her children Homewards, hath decreed
This Holy Season to their need :

Heavenwards, Homewards ! through the dense
Dark clouds of sorrow, and the sense
Of present frailty, past offence :

Heavenwards, Homewards ! by the road
The poor in spirit ever trod,
And tread, in pilgrimage to God.

Heavenwards, Homewards ! till they win
That blest inheritance, wherein
Is no more Sorrow, no more Sin.

                                   S. J. STONE.

SIXTH FRIDAY.

THE TWO GREAT COMMANDMENTS.

THE SECOND.

How contrary to nature! To love my neighbor as myself. Not my child — not my sister — not my dear, chosen, tender companion. But my neighbor, the human being with whom I come in contact: whose lot joins mine in any way: who can be affected by me or I by him. This person I am to love as myself. I am to be as tender of his reputation. I am to be as tolerant of his faults. I am to grieve over his misfortunes, to be glad in his prosperity; I am to pray for him to God, and to influence men to treat him kindly. Is he disagreeable to me? Repellant, trifling, unsympathetic? That does not alter his relation to me. Look at Christ's life. We are all very glad to feel He has loved us as Himself; that He is our Neighbor. Do we never seem trifling, repellant, unsympathetic to Him, in the midst of our sins and follies? Let us try at least for a shade of His charity.

(205)

The things that are hard to nature, are the things that grace loves to accomplish in our souls. The gospel says—

"Verily, verily, I say unto you, he that believeth on Me, the works that I do shall he do also; and greater works than these shall he do: because I go unto my Father. And whatsoever ye shall ask in *My Name*, that will I do, that the Father may be glorified in the Son. If ye shall ask anything in My Name, I will do it."

After this, if we have not courage, what could give it to us?—It is hard to flesh and blood, this second great commandment.—But it is not impossible to flesh and blood, or it would not have been given to us. Let us believe that we have the grace, after we have asked for it, and striven for it, and we shall have it. If we begin by small practical ways of unselfishness, always enlarging our sympathies by thought and mental effort, we shall find that this temper of benevolence will grow in us. It is very easy to notice in ourselves and others, the rapid growth of a bitter spirit that sets us daily more and more against every one around us: the other sort of spirit will perhaps grow and increase as surely, if we try the right means to foster it. By and by it may come to us to find it impossible to think harshly and angrily of any one. There are states of mind in which everything makes us happy; perhaps there may be a state of mind when everything will make us gentle and affectionate. It has been so with others in the strife, before us. Maybe they had no better hearts to begin with, than we have.—One thing is certain: this virtue grows with exercise. It is hard to feel no interest in a person you have benefitted: it seems to give you a higher ground to stand on, and his faults look so much less, seen from above.—And to pray for people, is to knit you very closely to them. Few things give one a greater feeling of interest in, of compassion for, of fellowship with another, than to have prayed for him.

———

Is thy cruse of comfort wasting? rise and share it with another,
And through all the years of famine it shall serve thee and thy
   brother;

Love Divine will fill thy storehouse, or thy handful still renew;
Scanty fare for one will often make a royal feast for two.

For the heart grows rich in giving; all its wealth is living grain;
Seeds, which mildew in the garner, scatter'd, fill with gold the
   plain.

Is thy burden hard and heavy? do thy steps drag wearily?
Help to bear thy brother's burden; God will bear both it and
  thee.

Numb and weary on the mountains, wouldst thou sleep amidst
  the snow?
Chafe that frozen form beside thee, and together both shall glow.

Art thou stricken in life's battle? Many wounded round thee
  moan;
Lavish on their wounds thy balsams, and that balm shall heal
  thine own.

Is the heart a well left empty? None but God its void can fill;
Nothing but a ceaseless Fountain can its ceaseless longing still.

Is the heart a living power? self-entwin'd, its strength sinks low;
It can only live in loving, and by serving love will grow.

AUTHOR OF SCHONBERG COTTA FAMILY.

SIXTH SATURDAY.

THE LAMB OF GOD.

"WHICH taketh away—or beareth—the sin of the world." This is a saying marvellous in our eyes and as incomprehensible as the doctrine of the Trinity, as the existence of evil—as the never yet unfolded secrets of life—of death—of resurrection. A great law is revealed to us, out of the clouds. We cannot see upon what it rests. We cannot reconcile it with any of our foundations of reason and justice. It was necessary for us to be told the law, just as it was necessary for the Jews to be told the laws of health (which mankind had not yet reached), to be preserved in the midst of the nations whose ignorance was destroying them. The great laws of the spiritual world are as unknown to us, as these laws were to them. Gradually when the mists fade away, and the light of eternity shines forth, we may see upon what this great law rests, upon what its fulfilment depends. Till then, we must simply believe, and be thankful.

14   (209)

that God has revealed even the giant outline of this stupendous Truth. Sin—penalty—expiation—pardon—The Lord hath laid on Him the iniquity of us all—The blood of JESUS CHRIST cleanseth us from all sin.

How much of this did the Baptist see, when he looked upon the Son of Man and exclaimed—"Behold the Lamb of God which taketh away the Sin of the World!" Prophets do not always know "half the deep thought they breathe." But he believed—whatever God showed him, and that was enough for his salvation, as thank God, it will be for ours. By searching we cannot find Him out; by worshipping we may.

———

We need not now like Israel's son
   The sprinkled ashes making pure;
For us a nobler work is done,
   And we have found a better cure.

Forth from the lone camp in the wild,
   A spotless thing without a stain,
They led th' unblemished creature mild,
   And slew her in the desert-plain.

Bring hither what your hands have spoiled,
   The gold, the silver, and the lead—

Or if there be whose robe is soiled,
  Or one whose hand hath touched the dead:

Come scatter wide the ashen shower,
  And let the waters o'er them lie,
And that bright sprinkling shall have power
  From aught unclean to purify.

A stainless victim, holy all,
  Without a spot on soul or frame,
Forth from the city's guilty wall,
  To death our sinless Offering came.

And lo! a tide to cleanse, and save,
  A thousand times more free and wide
Than that old purifying wave,
  Is gushing from His riven side.

That did but touch the outward part,
  This purifies the soul within:
The only tide to reach the heart,
  The only wave that washes sin.

Then if there be, who born anew,
  Have soiled the robe without a stain,
Come hither, and this crimson dew
  Shall wash it white as snow again;

And bring whate'er in studious hour,
  Whate'er in life's keen strife ye gain,
Learning, and wealth, and moral power,
  Each treasure of the heart and brain.

Bring burning thought, and reason strong,
  The iron of the earnest mind,
The golden pen, the silver song,
  Nor leave one glorious gift behind.

And wash them all in Christ's dear Blood,
  So shall your works be sanctified;
For naught is pure, or true, or good,
  That hath not touched that crimson tide.

                    CECIL FRANCES ALEXANDER.

PALM SUNDAY.

What do ye loosing the colt?—S. Mark, xi. 5.

IT was the day of the triumphal entry into Jerusalem; our Lord was on the way thither (how
often it is "on the way," in the gospel stories—
" by the road side,"—" as He went,"—"as they jour-
neyed "—how seldom as they sat ; how never in His
own house. Journeying ; never in a home, never
where we find our greatest rest and pleasure; by
the sea-side, by the road-side, in the desert, in
the wilderness ; crossing the fields of corn ; resting
beside the well at noon-day; very seldom we hear
of Him save under the open sky, and in God's
other temple. If He goes under a roof, it is to
work a miracle of mercy, to teach a sacred lesson :
think of our reposed, sheltered lives, the blessed
roof of home above us night and day, resting in
the dear familiar places that we love, after our
short absences and labors.) The two disciples
go to the village where they are sent. They come
to a place where two ways met; two ways, two

wide village streets perhaps, with people loitering about and children playing as in our village streets to-day. And before the door of a house at this corner where the two ways met, the disciples saw, as they were told they should see, a colt tied. And apparently without fear or hesitation, they went up to it, and unloosed it from its fastening. Then certain of them that stood there (the owners, says S. Luke) said to them, seeing the act "What do ye, loosing the colt." And the men intent on their Master's business return the simple answer:

"The Lord hath need of him."

And they let them go without a word of remonstrance. That would have surprised them very much perhaps, if they had not been too much occupied with their errand, and too much impressed with the infallibility of their Master's word. He had said it should be so,—and the surprise would have been if it had not come to pass.

Now in how far do we follow their example? How far are we impressed with the sacredness, the inviolability of every word that our Lord has spoken? How full of faith are we that what our

Lord lays upon us to do, we *can do* and must do, and shall not be hindered? O puny, sickly faith! What wonder that the world lays its hand upon our arm and stays it; and says with sneers, "Hath the Lord said? And who is the Lord that says?"

Somewhere, some one has written, "if Christians lived, for *one day*, up to their religion, the world would be converted before night-fall." Why might it not be? Think of the magnificent possibilities of our faith; think of the power of the Godhead which we are permitted to invoke; which is pledged to our assistance. Think of it, infinite power, and infinite truth, *pledged* that our prayer shall not return to us void. If we only *dared* do what we are bidden; if we were not afraid of the world, afraid of ourselves, and worst of all, afraid that God would not keep His promise to us; and that maybe after all, it was some great mistake. No; if we would simply go about our religious duties as if we believed in them, and were not ashamed of them; if when the Church and duty demand time and energy that the loiterers cannot understand, we should say bravely, the Lord hath need of them, we might not go away ashamed. If sacrifices, little and great, are done in that Name, people can understand, and will not interfere. There is a strange power in unfaltering confidence: the crowd gives way right and left, to the man that believes in himself. Who would not be ashamed of a servant that sidled and edged his way along, doubting of his message, distrusting its importance, vaguely afraid to disobey his master, faintly hoping it might come out all right?

Do we believe in the existence of a spiritual Kingdom, a life of supernatural power, the working of the laws of that life that are as inevitable as they are inscrutable? Let us live as if we believed so. Are we the regenerated sons of that Kingdom: are our children heirs with us of that unspeakable heritage? Let us believe this bravely and never fear for them, or for ourselves, that God will fail us. Do we feed upon the Eternal Sacrifice of the Body and Blood of our Saviour Christ? Let us never doubt or deny, by faint acquiescence or by careless preparation, that we hold that high and holy faith. Are all things possible to him that believeth? Is Christ able to save to the uttermost them that come to Him?

The life that we now live, can it be lived by faith in the Son of God? O endless, endless, list of promises and pledges. O wonderful life that lies within the reach of the Church, that she will not put out her hand to grasp! That she falters to unloose and lead away to serve her Master's march of triumph!

"He was wounded for our transgressions; He was bruised for our iniquities."

O Jesus, bruised and wounded more
  Than bursted grape, or bread of wheat,
The Life of Life within our Souls,
  The cup of our salvation sweet,
We come to show Thy dying Hour,
  Thy streaming Vein, Thy Broken Flesh;
And still the Blood is warm to save,
  And still the fragrant Wounds are fresh.

Oh, Heart that, with a double Tide
  Of Blood and Water maketh pure;
O Flesh once offered on the Cross,
  The Gift that makes our pardon sure;
Let never more our sinful Souls
  The anguish of Thy Cross renew;
Nor forge again the cruel nails
  That pierced Thy Victim Body through.

CECIL FRANCES ALEXANDER.

Soul of Jesu, make me holy,
Make me contrite, meek, and lowly;
Soul most Stainless, Soul Divine,
Cleanse this sordid soul of mine;
Hallow this polluted soul,
Purify it, make it whole;
Soul of Jesus, hallow me;
      Miserere Domine.

Save me, Body of my Lord,
Save a sinner vile, abhorred;
Sacred Body, wan and worn,
Bruised and mangled, scourged and torn,
Pierced Hands, and Feet, and Side,
Rent, insulted, crucified,
Save me—to the Cross I flee;   .
      Miserere Domine.

Blood of Jesus, Stream of Life,
Sacred Stream with Blessings rife,
From that Broken Body shed
On the Cross that Altar dread;
Given to be our Drink Divine
Fill my heart and make it Thine;
Blood of Christ, my succor be;
      Miserere Domine.

Holy Water, Stream that poured
From Thy riven Side, O Lord,
Wash Thou me without, within;
Cleanse me from the taint of sin,

Till my Soul is clean and white,
Bathed, and purified, and bright,
As a ransomed Soul should be;
   Miserere Domine.

Jesu, by the wondrous Power
Of Thine awful Passion hour,
By the unimagined Woe
Mortal man may never know;
By the Curse upon Thee laid,
By the Ransom Thou hast paid,
By thy Passion comfort me;
   Miserere Domine.

Jesu, by Thy bitter Death,
By Thy last expiring Breath,
Give me the eternal Life
Purchased by that mortal Strife;
Thou didst suffer Death, that I
Might not die eternally;
By thy dying quicken me;
   Miserere Domine.

Miserere: Let me be
Never parted, Lord, from Thee;
Guard me from my ruthless foe,
Save me from eternal Woe;
In the dreadful Judgment Day
Be Thy Cross my hope and stay;

When the hour of death is near,
And my spirit faints for fear,
Call me with Thy Voice of Love,
Place me near to Thee above,
With Thine Angel Host to raise
An undying song of praise ;
     Miserere Domine.
       O. O. P.

MONDAY IN HOLY WEEK.

———◆———

"Ought not Christ to have suffered these things and to enter into His glory?"—S. Luke xxiv. 26.

COMING into the annual darkness of this week, it seems sometimes as if the reproach might well be addressed to us; "O fools, and slow of heart to believe all that the prophets have spoken." It seems to us hardly as if it *ought* to have been; as if it were some strange and terrible casualty that had saved the world,—not the regular plan and purpose and unchanging law of God, in His heart from the beginning. Yes; Christ's sufferings have in a way opened the gate of His glory; enhanced the magnificence of His sovereignty. Since He has drunk of the brook in the way, He has lifted up His head in greater triumph. Are there laws that bind the Godhead even? The law of voluntary humiliation that leads to divinest joy? O fools and slow of heart to believe!—slow of hand to practise—slow of foot to follow. Humble thyself. Crush thy proud and bitter heart beneath the heavy and grinding stones of discipline; silence thy flippant tongue; deal hardly with thy lightest fault; sacrifice thy human wishes; learn to do with alacrity what is hateful to thee. Put others in place of self. Count the hours lost that thou spendest on thy comfort, thy pleasure, thy advantage. Suffer these things and see the glory thou shalt enter into. See it even here. The bright rays streaming out from those opening doors will reach thee, even here. The sense of triumph and of ecstasy will thrill thee, even here. The tender sympathy and gladness of thy Saviour's heart, will even here be felt.

———

"What came ye forth to see?
　The desert paths are drear;
　The desert air is still.
　What came ye forth to hear?
　A whisper 'mid the reeds,
　Or voice of one that pleads,
Persuading soft, or prophet's voice austere?"

"I came not forth to look
　For prophet or for seer,
　For word from lip or look
　I wait not, waiting here;

Where neither speech nor voice
Is heard, my spirit's choice
Abides, for unto me
The Lord hath show'd a Tree."

" What would'st thou with this tree,
Bare, leafless, gaunt ?   On thee
It drops no tendril now,
It stretches forth no bough.
Behold the woods, the summer woods are fair,
On Lebanon the oak
Stands with its heart unbroke
In giant strength ; what green leaves tremble there !
The very gourd that springs
And dies within a day,
Will spread its fan-like wings
To shade thee wh¹le it may;
The rose is sweet ere yet it pass away,
The lily blooms and fades in still decay.

" Thou lovest well the slow
Sweet lapse of running waters o'er the stone,
The song of birds at early morn, the low
Light ruffling winds ; what find'st thou here ? a moan;
What hearest thou ? a sigh
Half uttered 'twixt the sky
And earth, from age to age that seems to die.

" No bird upon this tree
Will sit and sing to thee ;

No flower will spring beneath; all hurry by
 That pass this place; the vine
 No cluster yields, for wine
None ask, and here the merry-hearted sigh."

 " Yet hence I will not stir:
 What healing gums distil
 From out this tree! Of myrrh
The mount is this, of frankincense the hill,
 And all around are fair
 Broad meads, with shepherds there
That feed and guard their flocks contented still.

 " By Sinai long I stay'd,
And heard a voice that spake to me, ' This do,
And thou shalt live;' but when more close I drew,
I saw with hidden fire the mountain shake;
Upon the air I heard the trumpet break
Long, loud and louder yet; what hope had I
When even Moses said, I fear and quake—
Let not God speak unto me, lest I die!

 " To Tabor then I came.
How fair, methought, how pleasant is this place,
How green and still! Then, Jesus, on Thy face
I look'd and it was comely; full of grace
And truth Thy lips as one whom God hath blest.

" Here then methought, for ever will I rest,
 Here will I build my shrine, and pay my vows;
  But while in sweet content
  To pluck fresh boughs I went,

Peter and James and John,
Yea, Jesus, too, had gone,
And I was left amid the wither'd boughs.

"At length another place
I reach'd at noon; the ground was bare;
Of a great multitude I saw the trace,
But all was silent now; no marvel there
    My eyes beheld, no law
    I heard, no vision saw,
Save JESUS only, Him the Crucified.
I saw my Lord that looked on me and died.

"Here will I see the day
    Pass by, the shadows creep
    Around me; here I pray,
        And here I sing and weep;
        Here only will I sleep
        And wake again; I keep
    My watch beneath this Tree
    The Lord hath show'd to me."

                            DORA GREENWELL.

15

TUESDAY IN HOLY WEEK.

LITTLE is said by St. John of the eating of the last supper, nothing of the institution of the Holy Eucharist. Writing later than the other Evangelists, he did not feel called upon to repeat that which they had described in full, and of which he had already spoken clearly, setting forth its doctrine in the Lord's own words, ch. vi., and which was set forth before their eyes, in word and action, at every celebration of the Liturgy. The beloved disciple tells us, as is his wont, more of the words of Jesus, and of the feelings in the Sacred Heart of the God-man. From him we learn how the Saviour, with all the weight of woe beginning to press upon Him in its heaviest agony, with the prospect of soon parting in bodily presence from the disciples and of entering into His glory, loved His own, as in the beginning, so now, and for evermore, even to the end.

It is but faintly that we can enter even into what we may call the human sorrows and cares of

(226)

the Son of Mary. Into those sorrows and cares which
He took upon Him by virtue of His being Son of
God we cannot enter at all, as when in the agony in
the Garden His soul was exceeding sorrowful even
unto death.   We can only stand afar off, won-
dering and adoring.   But in all, through that
mysterious agony, through the long hours on the
Cross, He loved and thought upon His own. So
also in His three days' stay in the resting-place of
the departed. So in the day of His Resurrection, as
when He sent His reassuring message to Peter.
Therefore we know certainly, that now, having
departed unto the Father, He yet loves His own
which are in the world, and will love them unto the
end.

He shows His love in His earnest desire to eat
this Passover with His disciples before He suffers.
One reason for this intense desire was, it seems, that
now for the last time He should be among them as
their friend and companion, eating and drinking
with them. For His Death and Resurrection made
a great change in their relations. He was anxious,
too, to fulfil the Law of Moses, anxious to have all
things done that He might the more speedily accomplish His Passion and His Cross. But most

especially He desired it, we believe, that He might give to them, as the representatives of His Church, the Sacrament of the New Covenant, the Sacred Mysteries of His Death, the Sacrifice forever, their continual Feast. Nowhere else is it told us that He desired anything with exceeding desire. This Passover He will eat now, and never more. For it shall be fulfilled, immediately, in the Kingdom of God. That cup He gives them, the wine mingled with water, the Cup of the Old Covenant at the Supper, of which He will not drink again. That too shall be fulfilled, immediately, in the Kingdom of God. He is about to give them the Flesh of a better Lamb, the Lamb of God, a better Cup, even the Cup of the New Covenant in His own Blood; broken and shed for them already in everlasting purpose, in type ; soon to be in very deed broken and shed upon the Cross.

When the Children of Israel entered into the promised land the Manna ceased (Josh. v. 10–12). So now that the disciples of Jesus are entering into the Kingdom for them the old order ceases. Shadows flee away. The substance is made theirs, the True Manna, the Bread from Heaven.

FROM " THE GOSPEL STORY."

"The Master sayeth, Where is the guest-chamber, that I may
eat the Passover with my disciples?"

———

Now Wisdom lifts on high,
Her voice,—abroad a summons clear she sends:
"Come hither, friends, and eat abundantly,
Yea, drink, beloved friends!

"My festal board is fair,
My banquet-chamber ready, on its chief
Long waiting, little need the heart prepare
To keep the feast of grief;

"My wine is mingled strong
With myrrh! full mingled is it, spiced and sweet;
This Passover with bitter herbs how long
Have I desired to eat.

"Come, eat my bread,—nor shrink
My soul's deep, secret baptism to share;
Be strong, beloved friends, the cup to drink,
My master's hand doth bear.

"Be patient! from the north
The wind blows keen, the garden little yields
Of pleasant fruits, yet hath our Lord gone forth
To walk among the fields.

"His steps have left the flowers,
He feeds no more among the lilies sweet,
A husbandman he toils through long cold hours,
With wounded hands and feet.

"Come reap with Him for white
These fields and ready, thrust the sickle in;
The harvest stands but thicker for its blight
    Of death, woe, want, and sin.

"Come, glean the blasted ear
With him, nor be the wither'd grass forgot
That waves upon the house-top thin and sere,
    By mower gather'd not.

"To many a marish place,
Choked with the living wreck that on earth's fair,
Cold bosom drifts awhile and leaves no trace,
    I bid your steps repair.

"Unto the darken'd mine
I call you now, unto the burning plain;
To cells where fetter'd spirits moan and pine,
    Where madness shakes its chain.

"I bid you to the drear,
Dark house, unloved of all, where want and age,
Sit day by day,—and turn without a tear
    Life's saddest, weariest page.

"In homes unblest, where care,
Grown fierce and reckless, turns at last and rends
The heart she broods on; I would meet you there,
    Oh, friends, beloved friends!

"I tryst with you! I bid
Two long predestined lovers, held apart
By seas, storms, graves,—by flaming swords,—unchid,
    Now seek each other's heart.

" Grief waits for love,— she turns
To that kind voice, nor will the stranger's hear;
Upon her worn and wasted cheek she yearns
    To feel love's burning tear.

" Love seeks out grief,—he knows
No lips save his in fondest ministering,
From out her rankling wound, ere yet it close,
    Can draw the deadly sting.

" He fain unto his breast
Would draw her aching brow; uncomforted
He knoweth she hath dwelt in long unrest,—
    She may not die unwed.

" Hear, Earth and Heaven, their vow!
Whom God hath joined in one let none divide;
Rejoice, O Heaven! be joyful, Earth, for now
    The bridegroom meets the bride!
                DORA GREENWELL.

———

Christ, who for Thy thirsting flock
Madest waters clear to flow,
When, with rod upon the rock,
Moses struck the wondrous blow;
Strike, O Lord, our stony hearts
With Thy Cross and with Thy fear,
Till from them in sorrow starts
Many a penitential tear.

Christ, who by Elisha's hand
Madest iron lightly swim,
When he, on the Jordan's strand,
Cast a sapling in the stream;
Cast, O Lord, Thy Cross of love,
When our hearts in sin lie drown'd;
So shall they return above,
So shall be the lost ones found.

Christ, Who by S. Peter's shade
Didst Thy glorious light reveal,
And the sick beneath it laid
Didst, O Great Physician, heal,
Let thy Cross' shadow rest
On each sick and wounded soul;
So shall we, dear Lord, be blest,
So from all disease be whole!

R. F. L.

WEDNESDAY IN HOLY WEEK.

On this day is commemorated the entering of Satan into Judas; the unlocking of his heart by that prince who had so long coveted the key. All through those years of service perhaps both masters had been watching him, had been drawing him. But now the moment of choice had come, "Choose you this day whom you will serve." And he chose. O God! Is it too late to say, have mercy on him! A being of flesh and blood, the son of a mortal mother, the companion of human and gentle and honest men, one of twelve, selected out of thousands that then walked in Jewry! The amazing capacities of the human soul for infamy or for glory! the marvel of being permitted such a choice—such a range of place. "One of you is a devil." "Now are ye the sons of God."

He communes with the chief priests and captains how he may accomplish the capture of his master. His master, so humble a citizen of that capital, that it was necessary to have a guide to them that took Him. We can hardly believe that He could have been mistaken for one of His followers, that any one could have looked upon Him and not have known Him. Alas! The eyes of all men could not see Him then, cannot see Him now. And they were glad; oh! unholy joy. And covenanted to give him money. Who would dare to love it? *And he promised.* There are so many things to be learned from this event. First, the pang this treachery caused our Lord; which puts Him in sympathy with us in our disappointed friendships, in our ill-requited loves. Second, the possibility of falling from the highest spiritual places, which should fill us with the deepest fear. Third, the dawning influence of avarice on the soul, against which we should ever pray, for we never know when it is beginning. Fourth, the Fact of Total Perdition—" Better for such a man that he had never been born. Better that a millstone were hanged about his neck and he drowned in the depth of the sea." What words for our loving Lord to utter. And souls of men may *Perish?* God alone knows what that means. If we could have one instant's vision flashed upon us of the course of a lost soul, oh! how it would quicken our litanies, how it would fire our prayers. Have mercy upon us and *Save us.* Whatever Perdition means, we need not perish, if we lay our sins upon the Lamb of God, sold this day for the Sacrifice. If we are baptized with the baptism that He was baptized with, if we feed upon His Flesh. If every day we pray to Him in His words. If every day we take up His cross and carry it through our miserable, humble, narrow path ; we *cannot* perish. We are safe. We have His word.

Lord of life ! can this be so ?
One of us the child of woe !
One of us who walk'd before Thee !
One of us who now adore Thee !
Search me, with a pitying eye ;
Lord have mercy, Is it I ?

I have heard Thy gracious voice
Bid the bruised heart rejoice,
Quell the storm of care and strife,
Bring the dying soul to life,
Make the blind to see the sky ;
Lord have mercy, Is it I ?

I have at Thy table fed,
Drank Thy cup and ate Thy bread,

Preach'd Thy cross from door to door,
Nursed Thy sick, and fed Thy poor,
Taught the babes Thou blest to pray—
Lord, am I the castaway ?

Lord, I will obey Thy will ;
Anxious spirit ! peace, be still !
Rest thee !   'Tis enough to know
Present weal, and present woe ;
Tempt not God in wrath to tell
What awaits thee, Heaven or Hell.

Pray Him rather not to look
In His seal'd and awful book,
Lest the day be dark and drear,
If it sink in blood and fear ;
And the night should wearier seem,
If it keep our souls from Him.

Pray—and let us thankful on,
Darkling till our race be run,
Though the clouds be glooming o'er us,
And the yawning tomb before us,
And we bear the cross of pain,
Sinking till the grave we gain.

Only when the storm of woe
Beats upon our fenceless brow,

When we fail our watch to keep,
When we slumber, faint, or weep,
Lord! in mercy, Lord, be nigh!
Warn us, rouse us—" Is it I ? "

ANON.

THE ATHLETES OF THE UNIVERSE.

" Destitute, afflicted, tormented ; of whom the world was not
worthy."—HEBREWS xi. 37, 38.

Their names are names of kings
Of heavenly line,
The bliss of earthly things
Who did resign.

Chieftains they were, who warr'd
With sword and shield ;
Victors for God the Lord
On foughten field.

Sad were their days on earth
Mid hate and scorn ;
A life of pleasure's dearth,
A death forlorn.

Yet blest that end in woe,
   And those sad days;
Only man's blame below—
   Above, God's praise!

A city of great name
   Was built for them,
Of glorious golden fame—
   Jerusalem.

Redeemed with precious Blood
   From death and sin,
Sons of the Triune God,
   They entered in.

So did the life of pain
   In glory close;
Lord God, may we attain
   Their grand repose!

               Amen.
                 S. J. STONE.

THURSDAY IN HOLY WEEK.

THE large upper room—the twelve—the disciple leaning on Jesus' breast—the awe of the servants who felt that some crisis in their Master's life had come —the exaltation and sublimity of the thoughts of the One who knew that the moment had arrived for which He came into the world. The disciple who loved, has remembered more than they all, of His words. What should we do without those sublime Recollections of S. John? A few verses dispose of the occurrences in the other gospels: S. John writes page after page of the dear, dear words. O how he loved them, how he lingered over them! What shall we do to earn the title of the disciple whom Jesus loved? Love Him ourselves. Love Him, think of Him, dwell on His words, lean on His breast, *love* Him. Not ask to "learn to love Him." How cold that must sound to Him. But ask Him to love us, to look at us, to lean towards us, to yearn over us. And if He loves us with that special,

(239)

tender love, the fight is fought, the victory won, the heaven is sure.   The one He loves cannot be lost.

Oh! beautiful saint! saint of love, not work! Saint of memory, not action.   Saint of the Euchar-ist, not the stake.   How didst thou win Him? What gained thee thy place?   Was it thy youth? Was it because thy mother brought thee and asked for thee that highest place?   Nothing that S. John asked ever was denied him.   His mother asked what it was not his Lord's to give; but surely it *was* given to him of the Father.   Surely he who leaned on Jesus' breast sits at His right hand in heaven— or will—when we drink the Fruit of the Vine new in the Kingdom of the Father, at the Blessed Eucharist of the Regeneration.

―――――

Truly we need to pray this prayer:

" Mercifully grant that we may both follow the example of His patience, and also be made partakers of His resurrection ; through the same Jesus Christ our Lord."

For what need of patience we shall have, if we have not had it yet.   What certainty of suffering

lies before us; what parting Passovers, what Geth-
semanes, what Calvaries. It behooves us, once a
year, to look upon the picture of our Lord's Passion,
for ours is coming. Surely,—as surely as the
coming of the Good Friday of this very week.
Think of the pangs that lie between now, and our
last hour. Think of the partings, of the pangs of
soul; of the strange tortures and mysteries of physical disease; of the stranger and more profound
mysteries of mental disorder; all these, in great or
less degree, are ranged along the pathway of our
progress, be it long or short, and wait to meet us
and join themselves to us as we walk. O such dark
places as we have to go through. Such hours of
suspense as are before us; such dreads; such
doubts; sick-rooms, death-beds; giving up of dear
ones; sinking alone into the cold black waters of
the unknown, or seeing those waters close one after
another over those we love.

And all this in a few little years. How fast the
years go. How but a moment it seems since last
Holy Week. And as certain as that to-day around
the table were gathered father, mother, husband,
wife, child, brother, sister; so certain, in a few of
these quickly revolving years, will all those pangs be

16

felt that must come in the unbinding of that tight-knit Sheaf. Yes; it is inevitable; it must be; it lies before us. Why do we not hungrily apply ourselves to the contemplation of what will be our only help in that dark time? Why do we not fling ourselves before His Cross, and gaze and gaze, and fill our souls with strength? What He has borne, we, in our weak, feeble measure, have got to bear ourselves. If we have filled our hearts with the thought of Him; if we have studied, hour by hour, the last days of His Passion; if we have thrown ourselves forward in imagination into those coming darknesses, as foreshadowed by His sufferings, we shall be better able to meet our hour and the power of darkness. It shall not come upon us unaware; and we shall feel the fellowship with Him that is the surest comfort.

"Who His own self bare our sins in His own Body on the tree."

O, to think of *that!* when pain in all its monstrous strength, fastens on you, to think of that, is to feel a thrill of courage. Pain, in one shape or another, fills fully half our lives. How could we pray to a God who had never agonized; a God who was in Heaven, and who had never worn our shape or walked our earth. Mysterious and terrible as suffering is, let us be patient, we who are cowards ; let us be patient, it is a bond He will not disallow. Maybe it is involuntary ; we would not have courage to take it up ourselves. He has forced us into His fellowship. If we can only be patient and not rebel, maybe it will, with His sufferings, be accepted as our ransom.

What is patience? What was His patience? Silence, Endurance, Submission. We are never satisfied with our patience. No doubt that is right. We should not be satisfied. But patience is not joyful, is not triumphant. One can be deeply sad, sorrowful even unto death, and yet be patient. One can look with silent reproach on those who betray and those who forsake, and yet be patient. One can faint and fall to the earth in utter weakness, and yet be patient; can put back the nauseous draught, and yet be patient ; can look with anguish upon those that must be left, and yet be patient. Yes, and can cry with a loud and bitter cry to Heaven, and yet be patient. And can yield up one's soul to God with cries and moans that rend the air, and yet be patient.

O my God ! Dear to me as is the height of Thy

majesty and purity, dearer to me is the depth, the abyss of Thy sufferings. In it I can hide, and be contented never to lift up my head; *Thou knowest.* Thou wilt not despise me for my suffering as others may. I am safe with God, if not with man.

"I am weary, Blessed Jesus,
 Faint and weary, sad and drear!
Nothing brings relief or cheers me,
 Life's a burden,—death a fear.

Thou wast weary too, my Saviour,
 Asking water for Thy thirst:
Was it brought at once, Lord, to Thee,
 Were not questions ask'd Thee first?

I would pray, but language fails me,
 Oft repeated words are vain:
I can only say "Lord help me,"
 Praises flow not forth in pain.

Did words fail Thee, Jesus, Saviour?
 Thrice Thou didst repeat the same,
In Thine Agony and Passion,
 Bleeding till an angel came.

I am lonely, Lord,—forsaken;
 Blessed Spirits draw not nigh:
Sorrowful—none come to strengthen,
 Sighing—but none heed the sigh.

Didst Thou tread alone the wine-press?
Was wrath poured upon Thy Head?
In Thy death wast Thou forsaken,
That Thou mightest raise the dead?

Raise me, Saviour, from this torpor,
Lift me from this living grave;
With Thy cords of love, Lord, draw me;
Draw me to Thyself and save.

Soft and still a voice came to me,
" Dost thou think thou art alone?
Know that I am ever with thee;
Is not all I have thine own?

" Art thou wounded, griev'd, forsaken?
Sacred is each wound and tear;
Ev'ry drop by Me is counted,
Ev'ry sigh is treasur'd here.

" In this fellowship of suffering
Thou partakest of My lot;
Watch with me, one moment longer,
Trust Me—I forget thee not."

Praise be unto Thee, my Saviour,
Tears of gladness dim my sight;
Through Thy fellowship with sadness,
Darkness is exchanged for Light.

M. T.

"The king also himself passed over the brook Kedron."—
2 Sam. xv. 23.

"When Jesus had spoken these words He went forth with His
disciples over the brook Cedron."

————

Like him that doth the picture find,
Of one beloved but long unseen,
And gazes until form and mien
Live once again before his mind:

So living on the page of truth,
Doth many a scene beloved shine,
And we have hung upon the line,
And haunts familiar from our youth:

And pictured every hill and brook,
Aud looked into the sky above,
Till as it is with those that love,
We seemed to know their very look.

We seemed to see the yellow moon,
To watch ourselves the drifting clouds,
That hurried by, or hung in shrouds,
Across the burning Eastern noon.

How many Christian hearts have met
Between that city and the hill,
And over Cedron's mournful rill,
And up the steep of Olivet!

How oft that low mount, green and brown,
To substance and to shape has grown,

Filled in with colors of our own,
And shadowed from the distant town.

Over the brook a weeping king,
Behind a weeping host has past;
A long shrill wail comes on the blast,
We hear the quivering olives ring.

The faithful people go before,
Lamenting loud their monarch fled—
Barefoot he comes, with covered head,
Feeling another sorrow more—

The grief that lay all deep and dumb,
Behind the grief that sobbed and burned,
The father's injured love that yearned
Still for his rebel Absalom.

Another King has crossed the flood !
How many wayward sons had part
To wound and break that loving heart,
Whose tears were drops of falling blood.

And what a pale and weary brow,
In that dark olive shade bowed down,
The King that never wore a crown,
For whom the thorns are weaving now !

O mount ! where David's bitter tears
Fell on the softly-shaded sod,
Where David's King, and David's God,
Strove with a whole world's weight of fears.

O wild, dark brook ! that heard the cry,
A people's mourning on the air,
That murmured to the thrice-told prayer
Wrung from a deeper agony :
Bid our vain hearts some shade to borrow,
From that great mystery of grief ;
Let swelling wave, and drooping leaf,
Teach us the worth and depth of sorrow.

Tears were in royal David's eyes,
Strong tears upon my Saviour's cheek,
And shall we shun with spirit weak,
All sadder, holier thoughts that rise ?

Musings that mar our lighter strain,
Of heaven, and hell, and sinners lost,
And of the priceless price they cost,
Heart-sorrow, death, and lingering pain ?

Nay let us find some dark sad hour,
When we may weep and think alone
Of Christ, and of the judgment throne,
Of death and sin's destroying power.

Befits us well the brook of tears,
Befits us well the olive-shade,
Who have so rarely, coldly prayed,
Have trifled with so many fears.

Who shareth thus his Saviour's woe,
Shall come as David came again,
But to a city where no pain
Can enter, and no tear can flow.

                    CECIL FRANCES ALEXANDER.

GOOD FRIDAY.

THE GAZE OF THE MULTITUDE.

"And sitting down they watched Him there."

Not eager, excited, maddened as they were when they surged around the judgment hall, in the morning, and cried, Crucify Him; but deliberate, cruel, easy, mocking. They sat down, they made comfortable their strong healthy limbs; then they *looked at Him*.

What is it to be looked at? The human eye has wonderful power; people tell us who have stood before great crowds, that to be in sympathy with all those faces is a marvellous experience. But what must the experience be, to be repelled, wounded, driven back, shocked—by every glance in every face that is upturned to gaze; to be out of sympathy with every eye one meets.

But there is something worse than this. Jesus is in His mortal agony; and they are gazing at Him. The *pains of death;* think; and

(249)

they are watching them. How few deaths are not watched tenderly! If never before, one is loved and ministered unto then. Everything is sacred ; if any gaze, it is with blinding tears, with hungry love, to catch the last light in the eye. But This Death. Ah! During some illness, some great period of suffering, how easy to remember the effect of some unsympathetic, cold expression—perhaps on the face of a nurse, perhaps on that of the physician—how it is resented. How one resolves impetuously, that face shall never approach my bed of suffering again ; it is hard enough to suffer ; one wants all the help of sympathy at such a time as this! Ah God! There never was but one such time as *this*, when in His own flesh He bare our sins in His own body on the Tree.

"His piercèd Hands in vain would hide
His face from rude reproachful gaze—"

Think of it: strètched there upon the cross, with every physical torture that can be conceived ; with the mysterious agony of Redemption being borne ; with the most appalling mental sufferings ;—forsaken of His God, and Alone among His brethren.

When scorn and hate, and, bitter, envious pride
Hurl'd all their darts against the Crucified,
Found they no fault but this in Him so tried?
"He saved others!"

Those hands, thousands their healing touches knew;
On wither'd limbs they fell like heavenly dew;
The dead have felt them, and have lived anew:
"He saved others!"

The blood is dropping slowly from them now;
Thou canst not raise them to Thy thorn-crowned brow,
Nor on them Thy parch'd lips and forehead bow:
"He saved others!"

That Voice from out their graves the dead had stirr'd;
Crush'd outcast hearts grew joyful as they heard;
For every woe it had a healing word:
"He saved others!"

For all Thou hadst deep tones of sympathy—
Hast Thou no word for this Thine agony?
Thou pitiedst all; doth no man pity Thee?
"He saved others!"

So many fetter'd hearts Thy touch hath freed,
Physician! and Thy wounds unstaunch'd must bleed;
Hast Thou no balm for Thy sorest need?
"He saved others!"

Lord! and one sign from Thee could rend the sky,
One word from Thee, and low these mockers lie;

Thou mak'st no movement, utterest no cry,
   And savest us.
      MRS. CHARLES.

———

"I, the Lord, have brought down the high tree, have exalted the low tree, have dried up the green tree, and have made the dry tree to flourish."—EZEKIEL xvii. 24.

———

Thou sign of all our loss,
Thou sign of all our gain,
O strange, sweet, solemn cross,
I hail thee! and again
I hail thee! here through pain
Joy breaks, Love conquereth,
And here through bitter death
The Lord of life doth reign.

Speak not unto me, Life!
Thy voice that loves and grieves
I hear; the gentle strife
Of birds among the leaves,
Fond tones that in their flow
Make sudden pause and grow
To sweeter silence; sound of summer rain,
And children's voices down the homeward lane
That pass; prayer's constant, low,
Sweet pleading voice I hear;
The blow, the scoff, the jeer,

The maddening whip, the clanking chain,
The bitter laugh far sadder than the tear,
All these alike are thine! I know
Not what thy language means, confused and vain;
Now let death talk with me, its speech is plain.

Now let death speak with me, *Thy* death, my God,
Thy words upon the cross were plain and few;
It is my brother's blood that from the sod
Cries out of better things than Abel's knew.
Through dark decay it pleads, through sullen care,
It wins a triumph over earth's despair;
It turns to truth Life's failing prophecy,
It tells us that the Lord of Heaven was brave
And strong, and resolute in love to save
The world that He had made, yet could but die!

Then let me also go
And die with Him! why strive I for this crown
Of fading leaves, desired of all below,
Love, pleasure, sweet content and fair renown?
Why weep for flowers that fell too soon to spread
And drink the glory of the summer noon,
Sweet buds of promise quickly witherèd
That died, unkiss'd of June?
Behold, my God doth choose
The thorn, the rose refuse;
Lord is He of delight
And gladness infinite,
Yet hath He pluck'd no flower from all that bloom,
But in our earth's fair garden made His tomb.

Hail, blessed Cross! how bold
Thou makest me! how strong! no more I weep
O'er giant cities now the dragon's fold,
O'er mighty empires breathed to dust away;
No more a tearful chronicle I keep
Of all that passes ere our mortal day
Hath pass'd; nor grieve that in earth's fruitful, deep,
Warm soil, my life hath struck but slender hold.
All things must change, and into ruin, cold
And darkness pass and perish, yet behold!
All fades not with the fading leaf!   To me
      The Lord hath shewed a Tree!

      And many a leaf on me
      Hath fall'n from off this tree
      Of healing power!   I know
      Not yet how near the skies
      Its lofty stem will rise;
      Nor guess how deep below
      To what drear vaults of woe
      Its roots will pierce; I see
      Its boughs spread wide and free,
      And fowls of every wing
      Beneath them build and cling.
      Hail blessed Cross! I see
      My life grow green in thee!
      My life that hidden, mute,
      Lives ever in thy root,
      When life fails utterly;
      All Hail, thou blessed Tree!

DORA GREENWELL.

A PRAYER FOR GOOD-FRIDAY.—SUNSET.

"Blessed Lord, with whom I have striven to abide this day, abide Thou with me in all the great and agonizing days of my life.

I have stood by Thy Cross while Thou hast suffered : stand Thou by me when I am suffering. Forget that I have been wearied and listless, and have in vain striven to keep my soul faithful. Forget that I have counted the hours long that I have spent by Thee. Remember only that I have striven, and that I have truly, truly loved, and that I have earnestly believed. Strengthen Thou the weak places of my soul; keep out the tempter now and ever. I have not listened to him. O my Lord, do not Thou listen to his accusations of me. Love me, for whom Thou wert willing to die. Bind my heart in strongest bonds of love to Thee, and make me willing to die for Thee. When I come to die, be Thou to me a friend and comforter ; do not leave my side for weariness ; for the calls of others who may say they need Thee. Do not count the hours long that Thou mayest watch me dying; shorten them in Thy great mercy, but do not leave me till I die. Give me visions of Thyself: O do not leave me nor forsake me. The dread of that day weighs upon my soul. Thou, who knowest what it is to be sorrowful and very heavy, lighten and take away that load, when the news is told me that I cannot live. O make that day Thine, as this day has been Thine. I have tried not to think my own thoughts to-day: O do Thou on that day give me Thy thoughts to think. I have fasted this day for Thee; do Thou on that day give me of Thyself to eat and drink. The sun has gone down and the Fast is over. When my last sun goes down, may my fast be ever over, and refreshment and perpetual light begin.—*Amen.*

From "MEDITATIONS for Holy Week."

———

Oh! that this day on which my Surety died
    May humble me, and out of Self and Sin
So draw me upward, that I may begin—
    Low at His Cross, exalted at His side,
Beneath my burden and above my pride—
    Henceforth a lowlier, loftier life, and win
The "Go up higher," and the "Enter in,"

Said only to the meek.   O Crucified !
Whom only thus I know as afterward
   Risen also and Ascended : let Thy pains
In Passion and in Death—while need remains—
   With all my life, borne for my sake, accord,
That I may rise o'er my dead self and be
   In heart, though here on earth, in Heaven with Thee.

S. J. STONE.

17

"AND they returned and prepared spices and ointments; and rested the seventh day according to the commandment."

Oh, that day of silence that comes after bereavement, that—

> "First great day of nothingness
> The last of danger and distress."

That sinking down in the hushed and darkened house; that feeling that we have wept all our tears, that we have prayed all our prayers, that we have said all our words to men, to God, and to our dead. That we can feel, can think no more. And we rest, according to the Commandment. The Commandment of Mercy planted in our nature. Blessed are those that can do it; that can yield to the power of the silent hours that the course of natural grief leads them to; can commune with their own hearts and be still in that awful Sabbath. No preparations, no fretting officious friendship; only silence, and God very, very near. There is a great strength

(258)

comes from this rest of the soul; all, all needed for the days to come. For our joys are not always so near as was the holy women's joy. One day more, how little they knew it, they were to hear again His dearest voice, look again into His living eyes. How little *we* know when we lie down, helpless, speechless, hopeless, unutterably weary, how near our joy may be. This is one of the blessed hopes of grief: that it may not be long. To meet our dead "we must plunge into Death and Eternity." But our longing finds no dread in that which in sunshine hours was a thought of terror. Our only dread lies in the long, long way through which our days may go before they are joined unto the Eternal Years of Paradise.

But may be it will be to-morrow that we shall see the face of our beloved in the Garden of Paradise. Sufficient unto the day is the evil thereof. Simple, simple rule. The earliest taught, the last learned. Holding its force alike in the little matters of daily business and in the great crises of our lives. We can bear the separation of to-day. Oh! but to-morrow, but the day following, but the dreary life ahead. Let us *trust* in *God*, and take to-day from His hand: to-day, that sacred ring of hours for which He pledges us bread, and strength, and deliverance. To-morrow we may see a vision of angels.

Sad, desolate women! That must have been a dreary Sabbath. But they rested; there was a Commandment. No doubt they longed to go to the grave, to weep there; to bear to that dearest spot the spices and ointments which they had prepared. But they remembered the Commandment. Even in that time of great amazement and affliction they held religiously and simply to the rules to which they were bound. In the torrent of strange and new emotion, that seemed sweeping everything away, they laid hold with simple faith of the one tangible, *right thing to do* that presented itself to their sight. And so, their Easter joy was full. Would it have been so if they had broken the Commandment, pleading the grand liberty of grand occasion? Would they have met the angels? Or would they have been repulsed and denied the sight of Him, as they were the touch of Him, even on the morrow?

———

A night of silence and of gloom:
My Master lieth in the tomb—
Mine was the sin and His the doom!

So on this awful eventide,
My self-trust gone, my wealth of pride
All spent and lost, I fain would hide.

And where?—Lo on this Eve alone
I come with contrite prayer and moan
And lay me down before the Stone.

All is so still, so deadly still—
E'en that dread scene upon the Hill
Scarce shook me with so strong a thrill.

For Calvary had its jeering crowd,
My tears were check'd, my love was cow'd,
My pride took courage 'mid the proud.

The soldiers sleeping heed me not,
Their vigil is perforce forgot;
The world is banish'd from the spot.

So here I weep—for none are near
To fill my craven heart with fear
Of some sharp gibe for every tear.

And the deep stillness hath a cry
Reaching my soul, and none are by
To drown it with their blasphemy.

It saith, "O ingrate heart, for thee
The passion in Gethsemane,
For thee the scourge, the mockery,

"The scarlet robe, the thorny wreath,
For thee the load He sank beneath,
For thee the Cross, the Cry, the Death!

"Yea, all for thee! and having learn'd
How great that love was, hast thou spurn'd
The due of gratitude it earn'd?

"Thankless and cold! thy broken vow
Of love and service asks thee now,
Here at His tomb, what doest thou?"

'Tis true—yet am I fain to come;
In grief I have no other home
But near Him, though 'tis near His tomb.

And as in self-convicted mood
On mine ingratitude I brood,
A voice upon the solitude

Breaks, like a benediction near,
And through the darkness, in mine ear
Whispers of Hope, and not of fear:

"Yea, all for thee! and all to save!
Forgives He not as He forgave?
Died His Love with Him in the grave?"

So on this holy eventide
I lay me down as at His side,
And pray to die as He has died:

That I may rise to meet the strife,
With this dead heart renew'd, and rife
With impulses of love and life.

But can it be with one so vain,
So weak, so fearful of disdain?
"It can be! by the right of pain,

And curse, and cross, and this dark night!
Thou shalt endure through all the fight,
And as thy days shall be thy might.

" So shalt thou bear His flag unfurl'd
'Mid ghostly foemen overhurl'd
In fearless love before the world ! "

Then, blessed Master ! only Friend !
Be near, inspire, sustain, defend ;
In prayer I battle till the end.

Till on this Lenten night forlorn
There breaks the final Easter morn,
And the unsetting sun is born.

So on this blessed eventide,
Here at Thy tomb, here at Thy side,
I lift one prayer, Abide, abide !

The old sweet prayer so earnestly
Pray'd one sad eve, and heard of Thee—
Abide with me, abide with me !

                                          S. J. STONE.

How doth death speak of our belov'd,
    When it has laid them low ;
When it has set its hallowing touch
    On speechless lip and brow ?

It clothes their every gift and grace
With radiance from the holiest place,
With light as from an angel's face.

Recalling with resistless force,
And tracing to their hidden source,
Deeds scarcely noticed in their course,—

This little, loving, fond device,
That daily act of sacrifice,
Of which too late we learn the price;

Opening our weeping eyes to trace
Simple, unnoticed kindnesses,
Forgotten tones of tenderness,

Which evermore to us must be
Sacred as hymns in infancy,
Learn'd, listening at a mother's knee.

Thus doth death speak of our belov'd,
   When it has laid them low;
Then let love antedate the work of death,
   And do this now.

How doth death speak of our belov'd,
   When it has laid laid them low;
When it has set its hallowing touch
   On speechless lip and brow?

It sweeps their faults with heavy hand,
As sweeps the sea the trampled sand,
Till scarce the faintest print is scann'd.

It shows how such a vexing deed
Was but a generous nature's weed,
Or some choice virtue run to seed;

How that small, fretting fretfulness
Was but love's over-anxiousness,
Which had not been had love been less;

This failing at which we repined,
But the dim shade of day declined,
Which should have made us doubly kind.

Thus doth death speak of our belov'd,
    When it has laid them low:
Then let love antedate the work of death,
    And do this now.

How doth death speak of our belov'd,
    When it has laid them low;
When it has set its hallowing touch
    On speechless lip and brow?

It takes each failing on our part,
And brands it in upon the heart,
With caustic power and cruel art.

The small neglect that may have pained,
A giant stature will have gained,
When it can never be explained;

The little service which had proved
How tenderly we watched and loved,
And those mute lips to glad smiles moved;

The little gift from out our store,
Which might have cheered some cheerless hour,
When they with earth's poor needs were poor,
But never will be needed more!

It shows our faults like fires at night,
It sweeps their failings out of sight,
It clothes their good in heavenly light.

O Christ, our life, foredate the work of death,
    And do this now;
Thou, who art love, thus hallow our belov'd!
    Not death, but Thou!

MRS. CHARLES.

————

What place is this forlorn,
A palace, or a prison, or a tomb?
What waste, wide world is this, what realm outworn,
    Compact of fire and gloom?

What aspects vast and drear
Are these that rise around, with eyes for hate
Too blank, that through the darkness search and peer,
    Fix'd in impassive Fate?

What sea is this? what shore?
What sullen, tidal moan that still recedes?
What waves are these that cast up evermore
    Weeds, foul and clinging weeds?

· Weeds, weeds around my hands,
Weeds, weeds around my heart, that choke and press,
And drag my spirit downwards unto lands
   Of dire forgetfulness.

Weeds, weeds about my head
Are wrapp'd, I said "The darkness covers me;"
But even while I spake, *among the dead*
   I knew my soul was free.

One cometh on the wings
Of morn, to Him the darkness is as light,
He seeks my soul, He saves it from the kings
   Of Hades and of Night.

He cometh, o'er my woes
A victor, purple in His garment's stain,
Red with the life-blood of His conquer'd foes
   And mine—death, sin, and pain.

As one that on the vine
Treads in the bursting wine-vat, He hath trod
The press alone, and trampled out a wine
   Ripe for the wrath of God.

He binds within His crown
The thorn that rankled with so sharp a pang,
Beneath His kingly heel He treadeth down
   The adder's piercing fang.

Before His breath the bands
That held me fall and shrivel up in flame.
He bears my name upon His wounded hands,
   Upon His heart my name.

I wait, my soul doth wait
For Him who on His shoulder bears the key;
I sit fast bound, and yet not desolate,
 My mighty Lord is free.

 Be Thou uplifted, Door
Of everlasting strength! the Lord on high
Hath gone, and captive led for evermore
 My long captivity.

 What though these rocks be steep,
The valley dusk, with crowding shadows dim,
Ere Tophet was of old made large and deep,
 I was beloved of Him!

DORA GREENWELL.

EASTER.

WHILE this is the greatest mystery connected with our bodies, greater even than the mystery of our creation and the mercy of our preservation, it is the one which we dwell on least for *ourselves*. But when the first parting comes on these mortal shores, and we see for the last time the one we have loved in the flesh, laid down in the "wormy bed"—; when the hideousness of corruption begins before our very eyes even in those short days;— oh, then we begin to think about the grand and beautiful words graven in the rock with a leaden pen forever; then we cling to the promises; then we read with a new meaning the majestic chapter in Corinthians that was said over the corrupting, changed dead flesh and bones that had been our happiness and love.

It is such a strain to poor, faint, mortal thought. We would never look over that giddy precipice into the tremendous spaces of eternity, if not to catch sight of something that we loved that had been swallowed up in the vast abyss.   And now *it concerns us*, and we bend our thoughts on that which is impossible of comprehension, and learn to believe that which seems past believing.   That we shall come again; "that in our flesh we shall see God;" that *our eyes* shall behold and not another; that the perished flesh shall live, in some way—a better way; and that when we awake up after His likeness we shall be satisfied with it. A spiritual body.   What must that be!   A day on which death and time are conquered; what must that glory be!   The body safe—the poor body! and no longer an enemy to the struggling soul.

I. MARY MAGDALENE ON EASTER MORNING.

'Last at the Cross and first beside the Tomb:'
    Love ere the dawn had been her guiding ray,
And now the twain had come and gone their way
    Love still shone out amid the deeper gloom
Of that new loss which seemed a second doom.
    There last He lay: Love whispered, 'Linger there,'
And e'en in Hope's eclipse forbade despair,
    And could the dismal vacant depth illume.
There lo, the gleaming Angels! and the word,

'Why weepest Thou?' Yet was she all unmoved.
Angels sufficed not for the Form she loved,
  Nor all their glory for the stricken Lord.
Herein was love; Not Heaven itself can bring
Requital for the vision of its King.

II. THE GARDENER.

She turned, and knew Him not. So dim her eyes'
  With their long weeping; or not all withdrawn
Yet hung the veil before the face of dawn;
  Or was she holden from the blest surprise?
Howbeit, she knew Him not, and in surmise
  Saw but the Gardener; for around the tomb
The garden-plots were breaking into bloom,
  As Spring o'er prostrate Winter 'gan arise.
'With Spring he comes,' she thought, 'to train and tend
  And to subdue.' Erring she did not err:
The spiritual winter here had end,
  And Spring was come for all the world and her.
And He, the Gardener of the quick and dead,
In this new Eden bruised the Serpent's head.

S. J. STONE.

III. THE GREETING.

He said unto her, "Mary." With one cry,
  And in one moment, she was at His feet.

Oh to her desolate, thirsting soul how sweet
 The calling! as to those in days gone by
His voice on the dark waters, "It is I."
 O great good Shepherd! so He came to meet
The sheep that cried to find Him—so to greet
Her for whose need He was unseen so nigh.
 He knows His sheep and calls them all by name;
They hear not others but His voice they Know:
 She heard and knew the calling sweet and low,
And to His feet in reverent rapture came.
 O my great Master! thus and evermore
Thee would I seek and find, love and adore

"Thou, that on the first of Easters,
 Came'st resplendent from the tomb,
Leaving all thy linen cerements
 Folded in the cavern's gloom,
Come with Thine "all hail" to greet us,
 Come our Paschal joy to be;
Let our Altar, clad in brightness,
 Yield a Throne of white for Thee.

This shall crown the Queen of Sundays;
 Grant but this, our cup runs o'er;
Hymns that welcomed in thine Easter
 Made us long for this the more:
All the Paschal Alleluias
 Craved to see the Lamb appear:
Come the hour when Faith shall tell us,
 He is risen; He is here.

Thou, whose all transcendant Manhood,
 Knew not aught of bonds imposed,
Rising ere the stone was lifted,
 Passing where the doors were closed,
Present here in very essence,
 Is there aught too hard for Thee?
Fill us with Thy Light and Sweetness,
 From our darkness make us free!

Agnus Dei, we are guilty:
 Panis vitæ, we are faint;
But thou didst not rise at Easter
 To be deaf to our complaint;
Come, oh come to cleanse and feed us
 Breathing peace and kindling love,
Till Thy Paschal Blessing bear us
 To the Feast of feasts above."

O happy Flowers! O happy Flowers!
How quietly for hours and hours,
In dead of night, in cheerful day,
Close to my own Lord you stay,
Until you gently fade away.
O happy Flowers! what would I give
In your sweet place all day to live,
And then to die, my service o'er,
Softly as you do, at His door.

O happy Lights! O happy Lights!
Watching my Jesus live-long nights,
18

How close you cluster round His throne,
Dying so meekly one by one,
As each its faithful work has done.
Could I with you but take my turn
And burn with love of him, and burn
Till love had wasted me, like you,
Sweet Lights! what better could I do?

                              F. W. FABER.

Jesus, gentlest Saviour!
    God of might and power!
Thou Thyself art dwelling
    In us at this hour.

Nature cannot hold Thee,
    Heaven is all too straight
For Thine endless glory,
    And Thy royal state.

Out beyond the shining
    Of the furthest star,
Thou art ever stretching
    Infinitely far.

Yet the hearts of children
    Hold what worlds cannot,
And the God of wonders
    Loves the lowly spot.

As men to their gardens
  Go to seek sweet flowers,
In our hearts dear Jesus
  Seeks them at all hours,

Jesus, gentlest Saviour!
  Thou art in us now;
Fill us full of goodness,
  Till our hearts o'erflow.

Pray the prayer within us
  That to heaven shall rise;
Sing the song that angels
  Sing above the skies.

Multiply our graces,
  Chiefly love and fear,
And, dear Lord! the chiefest,
  Grace to persevere.

Oh, how can we thank Thee
  For a gift like this,
Gift that truly maketh
  Heaven's eternal bliss.

Ah! when wilt Thou always
  Make our hearts Thy home?
We must wait for heaven,—
  Then the day will come.

Now at least we'll keep Thee
  All the time we may;
But Thy grace and blessing
  We will keep alway.

                    F. W. Faber.

EASTER MONDAY.

PERSEVERANCE.

PERSEVERANCE is the one virtue without which no saint ever reached Heaven. Perhaps except the penitent thief—for he is the only saint *of moments* that we read of. His marvellous faith no doubt stood him in place of all other virtues. Some one says he was probably at that dark moment, when he made his confession, the only being on the face of the earth, who believed in our Lord's Divinity. His moments of sublime faith are counted to Him for years of patient perseverance no doubt. What virtue is harder to practise; for one cannot act it as a distinct virtue, it is made up of so many: of patience, and faith, and love, and above all, of hope. It is the steady grasp with which we lay hold of our guide; it is the clear eye with which we look ahead; it is the calm brain with which we judge between Earth and Heaven. It is the virtue that stoops to little wearying details; that does not live on ecstasies; that does not faint for often-time in-

(276)

firmities; that counts a fall but an incident of the way; that looks upon rapture of devotion as a gift of God, and does not murmur when the gift is gone; that sublimely hopes, that humbly prays, that religiously intends. Great King of unchanging purpose—grant us with all Saints, Perseverance!

Lent is over; the rebound comes. The good desires were God's gift and came easily; the good effects are harder to be worked out, with the world rushing in like a flood, and business, and pleasure, and all life to obliterate the good of our long fast. All experience shows us it is easier to be devout in days of sadness than in days of joy. And now comes the real trial; if a blessing is to crown our Lent, we must make these, religious days too, and keep a double guard on heart and lip, till the shock of the change has passed, and the course of our lives has settled down into the ordinary. And then, and ever, watch and pray, and strive. It is so hard to make those worn words fresh and strong. But they are so true, and no words mean the same. We must *never* stop our watch, we must *ever* pray. Oh that is the very breath of perseverance. Without prayer perseverance dies. And there is an end of striving. Ah! "Consider Him that endured such contradiction of sinners against Himself, lest ye be wearied and faint in your minds." What must we expect! The servant is not above his Lord. Contradiction of sinners; contradiction of our own hearts; contradiction of those who think they love us; contradiction of the malicious enemy. Good and powerful God! Leave us not neither forsake us, oh God of our salvation.

"Let no man think, that sudden in a minute,
　all is accomplished and the work is done;—
Though with thine earliest dawn thou shouldst begin it
　scarce were it ended in thy setting sun."

Oft when with icy heart, and dry
Affection's cold and tearless eye,
Barren as a desert, chilled as steel,
We at God's holy Altar kneel—
Still, while we persevere, and bear
With firm resolve, th' unlively prayer,
To holy sufferance will come
An answer from our Heavenly home.

For oft amid the weary crush,
The springs of Grace, with sudden rush,
Will overspread the rocky breast
With verdure new and dews of rest,

Filling the longing heart's distress
With floods of love and happiness,
One draft of which will countervail
Long days of want, and nights of wail.

Ah, ye who sit beneath the cloud,
And mourn for absence, deep, not loud,
Know this, that he who meekly bows—
And silent, grieves his absent Spouse—
One unexpected day shall feel
How good it was for him to kneel,
And mourn a temporary loss,
Under the shadow of the Cross.

For ah, what words of best desire,
What eloquence or Angel fire,
May tell the length, or breadth or height,
The richness of extreme Delight,
Reserved for him, who meekly bends,
Rather for love, than lively ends,
Who, unrequited, perseveres,
And labors still, albeit in tears.

W. C. C.

EASTER TUESDAY.

———◆———

S. JOHN XXI.

It was on the Sea of Tiberias. The seven
disciples mentioned in the story had gone out on
their fishing boat, led by S. Peter. It is easy to
imagine the strange unsettled feeling that they
had, between the Resurrection and the Ascension
Days, and before their commission had been given
them. And when S. Peter, wearied perhaps with
his strained feelings and uncertain life, exclaimed
with sudden energy "I go a fishing," they say to
him "We also go with Thee." It is such a relief, sometimes, to set one's self about anything
that looks like work, and promises to engage the
mind. But all that night they toiled in vain,
and the morning came, and they had taken nothing. When the daylight shone it showed them
Jesus standing on the shore. (Perhaps he had
been with them all through their dreary night
of labor though they had not seen Him.) Even
now they knew Him not. He asked them—

"Children, have ye any meat?"

They answer, " No."

Then He tells them to cast the net on the right side of the ship, for they should find. They obeyed Him, and now they are not able to draw it for the multitude of fishes. At this moment S. John, again, as at the sepulchre, first to discern, but not the first to act, says to S. Peter, " It is the Lord."

S. Peter, ever an enthusiast and ever foremost among his fellows, hearing this, goes eagerly beyond them all; girding his fisher's coat upon him, he casts himself into the sea. The ship is near the land (two hundred cubits off), the others follow in some smaller boat, but S. Peter is at the Lord's feet before them. They could never have forgotten that scene; the lonely shore, the early morning light, the sacred figure of the Crucified, standing there alone, with the mysterious shadow of His awful death still shrouding Him; their beloved, their own, the " human-hearted man they loved," their master, their companion, " the Lord," and yet—and yet. So ineffable, so awful, so undefinable is the separation between the living and those upon whom death has passed; they durst not ask Him,

" Who art Thou ? "

Knowing that it was the Lord, and yet, per-haps, feeling in their hearts, a vague uncertainty and awe—" this is, and yet this is not, He—" They saw as they came to land, a fire, and fish laid thereon, and bread. JESUS commanded them to bring of the fish which they had caught. Then, graciously, He cometh, and taketh bread and giveth them, and fish likewise. It must have been a strange feast, that early morning breaking of bread on the sea-shore, with the Man who had died and been buried, and was alive again, all within the waning of a single moon, or less. What awe should fill our hearts when *we* meet Him at the table He has set—in those early mornings, when the world sees Him not, as it saw Him not on the Tiberian shore. Our Risen Lord is with us. Let us say with S. John, " It is the Lord." Let us cast ourselves at his feet with S. Peter, and dare to claim Him and to serve Him, and to love Him ever.

———

It is a day of fear ;
Rise up betimes, go forth alone
With tongue fast sealed and heart bowed down,
Because Thy Lord is near.

Leave not thy thoughts to roam
Hither and thither where they would ;
Lest fretful cares on thee should crowd
Forgetful of thy Home.

Let not thine eye go free ;
Look on the earth beneath thy feet,
The pit that for thy sins was meet,
Had God been just with thee.

Bethink thee of thy sin ;
A stifling cloud, a festering sore,
A rotting canker at the core,
That gnaws thy heart within.

Good art thou to the sight :
But would thy cheek be dry as now,
As gay thy smile, as bright thy brow,
If all were brought to light ?

Yet not in gloomy sadness
Be thy heart bowed and eye down cast;
Is not the night of sorrow past ?
Is't not a morn of gladness ?

Think on the Holy Feast,
On His dear Love and gracious Name,
Who sanctifies Himself, the same
Both Sacrifice and Priest.

Go, and be One with Him;
Dwell thou in Him, and He in thee,
Him freely love Who sets thee free,
    Though but in shadow dim.

For, it shall not be so
In that great Day, when faithful Souls,
Whom flesh doth sway and sin controls,
    As they are known shall know:

To be for ever One
With Him, Whom with the Father High,
And Spirit, Angels tremblingly
    Adore as God alone.

Bless, Lord, Thy Child, oh bless;
Strengthen my weakness; soothe my grief;
Forgive and help mine unbelief;
    Restore my faithlessness.

To God, Whom all adore,
The Father, Son, and Comforter,
Who is before all creatures were,
    Be Glory evermore.

                              W. G. TUPPER.

———

Oh, weak are my best thoughts, and poor
    Is all that I can say;
Whether I lift my voice in praise,
    Or kneel me down to pray.

Wherefore I thank Thee, Gracious Lord,
　Whose love provides for me
A higher, and more perfect way
　Of drawing nigh to Thee—

The Way of Sacrifice—ordained
　When earth was in its prime,
Used by the hoary Patriarchs
　All through the olden time.

To Israel's Children in the Law
　Of trembling Sinai given ;
To us in later days confirmed
　By Christ Himself from Heaven.

O sweet ecstatic thought, 'tis mine
　To offer, as of yore,
A Sacrifice, and One in Power
　Excelling all before.

For me, upon an Altar fair,
　Is pleaded, day by day,
The Body and the Blood of him
　Whom Heaven and earth obey.

For me is immolated still,
　Again and yet again,
In the pure Host, the Very Lamb
　On Calvary's Altar slain.

And as the scarcely buoyant plank,
　Knit in the vessel's side,
With ease careers across the waves
　O'er leagues of ocean wide,

So, too, though weak my prayer, O Lord,
  Though poor my praises be,
Yet knit with this high Sacrifice,
  They win their way to Thee.

                              E. CASWALL.

THE END.